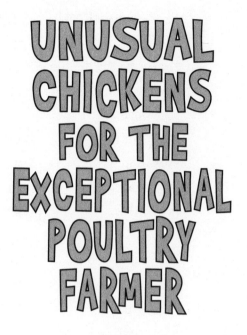

UNUSUAL CHICKENS FOR THE EXCEPTIONAL POULTRY FARMER

UNUSUAL CHICKENS FOR THE EXCEPTIONAL POULTRY FARMER

BY KELLY JONES

ILLUSTRATED BY KATIE KATH

Alfred A. Knopf · New York

THIS IS A BORZOI BOOK PUBLISHED BY ALFRED A. KNOPF

Visit us on the Web! randomhousekids.com

Educators and librarians, for a variety of teaching tools, visit us at RHTeachersLibrarians.com

Library of Congress Cataloging-in-Publication Data
Jones, Kelly (Kelly Anne).
Unusual chickens for the exceptional poultry farmer / by Kelly Jones ; illustrated by Katie Kath. — First edition.
p. cm.
Summary: Through a series of letters, Sophie Brown, age twelve, tells of her family's move to her Great Uncle Jim's farm, where she begins taking care of some unusual chickens with help from neighbors and friends.
ISBN 978-0-385-75552-8 (trade) — ISBN 978-0-385-75553-5 (lib. bdg.) — ISBN 978-0-385-75554-2 (ebook)
[1. Chickens—Fiction. 2. Farm life—California—Fiction. 3. Letters—Fiction. 4. Supernatural—Fiction. 5. Racially mixed people—Fiction. 6. California—Fiction.] I. Kath, Katie, illustrator. II. Title.
PZ7.J720453Unu 2015
[Fic]—dc23
2013050736

Printed in the United States of America
May 2015
10 9 8 7 6 5 4 3

First Edition

For everyone who supported me along the way
—KJ

Redwood Farm Supply

Unusual Chickens
for the Exceptional
Poultry Farmer

Write now to receive a free copy of our catalog:
Redwood Farm Supply
Gravenstein, CA 95472

Blackbird Farm

June 2, 2014

Mr. or Ms. Catalog People
Redwood Farm Supply
Gravenstein, CA 95472

Dear People Who Send Catalogs to People on Farms,

My great-uncle Jim had your flyer in his barn. I can't ask him about it, because he died a couple of months ago. But we live on his farm now, and if I have to live on a farm, I think it ought to be an interesting one, with chickens and ducks and maybe some peacocks or something. Right now, we don't even have tomatoes, just rows and rows of grapevines. And they don't even have grapes yet.

I can't find your website anywhere, so Mom said I should write you a business letter and request a catalog. Your flyer says you have Unusual Chickens for the Exceptional Poultry Farmer. I don't know what would make a chicken unusual, so maybe you'll send me your catalog and then I can stop wondering about them.

I do think you should know I'm a very responsible twelve-year-old. I did all my own packing and unpacking when we had to move. And I would be a good farmer—I always get A's on science projects, and I never forget

1

to water my bean seed or anything. Also, I know how to make French toast and pancakes without catching anything on fire or burning myself or melting the spatula. Unlike my dad. So you can see it would be handy to have chickens and a cow and whatever flour comes from. They would need to be cheap, though. We haven't got much money.

Thank you for considering my request. I look forward to hearing from you at your earliest opportunity.
(I think Mom must have found me some old letter format, because no one talks like this. If I did this wrong, it isn't my fault.)

Sincerely,
Sophie Brown

Mariposa García González
Heaven

Querida Abuelita,

I know you're dead, and I don't believe in zombies, so you don't need to write back or anything. I just wanted to write to someone. Kind of like a diary, only what does a diary care what I think? You might be dead, but you're still my grandmother and you still love me. No one writes back anyway, not even LaToya, even though she promised she would. I guess Katie was right when she told LaToya she'd have to be her best friend now, since she'd never see me again. LaToya didn't say anything back, and she didn't look at me, and she doesn't answer my emails either. That's not what I'd call a best friend.

We live on Great-Uncle Jim's farm now, far from LA, so I couldn't go see you even if you were still alive. It's okay here, I guess. We have a whole house of our own, way bigger than anyone's apartment, and a barn too, and a place that's sort of like a garage for tractors. But we barely fit, because Great-Uncle Jim saved a whole lot of things, just in case of who knows what. We made enough space in the attic for my bed, and if we clear some more things out, I will have a huge room up there.

I thought we were moving to a real farm, but it's more like a big, boring garden. Dead-looking grapevines and blackbirds and junk piles and bugs, that's it. The barn isn't red, like I thought barns were; where it isn't painted, it's just really old brownish-gray wood. It's kind of neat inside, though. A ladder goes up to what Mom says is the hayloft. Don't worry, it isn't falling down or anything. It's really peaceful, like a library, with a high ceiling and dusty old wood, and it smells like a pumpkin patch. It makes me think of horses sleeping.

The hayloft doesn't have any hay in it now. It's filled up with old furniture and dust and things in wooden boxes and under plastic tarps. I found this typewriter up here, and a desk, and I moved things around very carefully until I could sit here and type. It reminds me of your old typewriter, the red one you used to let me play with, the one Mom learned to type on when she was little. I was glad I still remembered how to put the paper in, and that the ribbon wasn't all worn out yet. When I hear that clicking, it always makes me think of you.

Dad said it would be really quiet here, but he must have remembered it wrong. When I open the big wooden shutters in the barn loft, I can hear weird animal noises from the farms all around during the day, even though they're really far away. Kind of like the zoo. Who knew cows would be that loud? There's no glass in the window (maybe it broke, and Great-Uncle Jim couldn't afford to fix it?), just a big open space. With the shutters open, I can look out down the driveway at the street, and hear the birds making a racket.

I'm careful to always close them when I leave the barn, so it doesn't rain on my typewriter, and so no animals get in. A couple of times today I thought I saw something black run behind a junk pile really fast. A sort of medium-sized something, like a cat, but as fast as a fast car. Just a black streak, really. When I told Dad, he said maybe it was a raccoon. Mom rolled her eyes and said she's never seen a super-speedy raccoon.

I miss LA. There aren't any people around here— especially no brown people, except Gregory, our mailman. (I like Gregory. He reminds me of Mr. Hightower, my teacher last year. They don't really look alike, but they're both tall black guys, and when they smile at you, it makes you feel like you did a great job on your science project or your letter or whatever, even if you didn't win a prize. I wish there were more people like Gregory here.) Dad fits in fine, but Mom and I don't.

I thought Mom didn't care where she lived, as long as she had her computer and printer and me and Dad, since she always begs everyone to just leave her alone so she can write (at least when she's on deadline, and she's always on deadline since Dad lost his job). But Sunday

afternoon, when all my aunts and cousins and everyone
except us would be heading to Tío Fernando's to cook
and eat and eat even more and then dance it all off,
I saw her in the hallway just staring at Great-Uncle Jim's
really ancient phone. She looked sad.

I miss you a lot, Abuelita. I miss everyone.

Te quiero,
Soficita

Mr. or Ms. Catalog People
Redwood Farm Supply
Gravenstein, CA 95472

Dear People Who Apparently Don't Actually Send
Catalogs to People on Farms,

Mom always says it's a bad idea to tell people what you
think while you're angry. But I bet I'm going to be angry
for a long time, so I don't see any point in waiting. Maybe
you think I'm just a kid with no money, whose parents
probably won't let her have chickens anyway. Maybe you
think sending me a catalog would be a waste of paper.
But I know my letter got to you, because Gregory, who
delivers our mail, said he would take it to your farm,
even though there was no street number on the flyer or
anything, and that was the way some farms worked.
Gregory is not the kind of person who would get that
wrong—he's got his whole sleet and snow and rain
commitment, and he takes that stuff seriously. Gregory
has never, ever been late with our mail.

Maybe if you had sent me a catalog, I could have
started working on getting my parents to agree to

some chickens. I'm good at planning ahead. Don't you ever worry that kids might not grow up to be farmers anymore, or that even if they do, they won't buy your special chickens because you won't even write back? Maybe you should think about planning ahead too.

Sincerely,
Sophie Brown

NOW!

SAFETY SOPHIE

always gloved, always goggled!
100% guaranteed

Blackbird Farm

Mariposa García González

A Better Place Than This Farm

Querida Abuelita,

I know you hate it when I mope around, and even though you're dead, I don't want you to be mad at me. So today I decided to explore for real.

I can't leave the farm without telling Mom or Dad, and they haven't been in very good moods lately, and the street in front of the farm is a highway. (But it only has one lane each way, so it's not a freeway, even though cars can drive fast on it—did you know that could happen?) Besides, everything is far away and there aren't any sidewalks or buses. I miss the beach. So I just explored the farm.

Here's the thing: Dad told me the other day that the last time he was here, when he was a teenager, his uncle had chickens and ducks and geese and even goats. He started to say we could make it all like it used to be. Then he saw Mom's face and remembered we're broke and that he's trying to find a job, and stopped. But all those animals had to live somewhere. I decided to look around and see if there was anything left from the real farm this was back then. Because let me tell you, Great-Uncle Jim never threw anything away.

So first I walked all the way around the edge of the farm. I started back behind the barn, in the part with all the big trees and acorns. From the highway, it looks like a wrinkle in the hills, or like the space in between fingers in a fist. (Sometimes, if I look far up one hill from the highway, I see a brown horse standing in the grass! We don't know those farmers yet, though, so I can't go explore up there.)

There's an old fence back there, so you can figure out which part is our farm and which part isn't. I followed the fence back behind that garage building, through lots and lots of trees and around blackberry bushes, and hopped over some rocks to get across the little creek. Then I walked out of the wrinkly hilly part and out of the trees and into the bright dusty sun, around all those rows of grapevines, following the fence down near the street.

There are rows and rows and rows of grapevines on both sides of our driveway, and lots of plants in between them that Dad says are weeds and aren't supposed to be there. I like the patterns that all the rows make when you walk by them. It doesn't smell like grapes out there, just like dust. But, if you look hard, sometimes you see little tiny green balls that Dad says will turn into real grapes eventually.

I walked for a long time, more than an hour, and ended up all the way back behind the barn again. Then I kind of felt more like I knew where I was. I picked some flowers and put them in a jar for my desk and some in another jar for Mom's desk too. At first I worried that they might belong to somebody, but then I remembered that the farm is ours, so these flowers must belong to us too. I'll give them to her later, when she takes a break.

The creek is pretty neat. I could hear the water and I kept wondering what that sound was, and then suddenly I saw it, running down the hill and over some rocks. I never thought I would have a yard with a creek and big trees and blackberry bushes. Our apartment building in LA had a few pots with some flowers and a big old lemon tree, but that was it. Here, there's so much dirt that you could probably plant fifty bean seeds and no one would even notice. I don't know what most of the trees and plants are, but there are a lot of them. I should get a book about them from the library.

But that whole time, I only saw one other house, way across the vineyard. Mom still makes me wear my whistle all the time, but how am I going to get mugged or kidnapped if there aren't even any people around? The only person I saw all day, aside from Gregory the mailman (I do like Gregory), was my dad.

Dad was trimming a grapevine. He had his gloves and Great-Uncle Jim's special pruners. "You can see

these are totally overgrown," he told me, showing me
how our grapevines had long green stems springing out
everywhere and getting in the way, but the ones over
the fence on our neighbors' vineyard kept their vines to
themselves. Then he started pruning one. "Uncle Jim
should have pruned them back when spring started, but
he probably wasn't up to it by then."

The grapevine he trimmed was looking pretty good
until I noticed clear sticky stuff oozing out all over from
everywhere he cut. "Dad, is it supposed to do this?" I
asked.

He took a look. "I'm not really sure," he said quietly. So
we both went and peered over the fence at the neighbors'
grapevines. I didn't see any sticky stuff on theirs.

"Should we ask Mom about it?" I asked.

He thought about it. "Better not interrupt her right
now," he said, and sighed.

So Dad decided to take a break and walk back up to
the house with me. On the way, he showed me a plant
called poison oak that makes you itch all over if you
touch it, and told me to keep an eye out for snakes. He
says they like to lie in the warm sun, and sometimes they
fall asleep and get surprised when you accidentally wake
them up. But most of them aren't poisonous, except for
the rattlers. When he went off to work on his résumé, I
decided to stay out of the plants and the sunny places for
the rest of today while I get used to things around here.

So I went to have a look in the building that's kind of like a garage. Inside, I saw the tractor and something else with wheels that none of us are sure what it is, not even Mom, and more of Great-Uncle Jim's junk that's metal. Dad says it's where Great-Uncle Jim used to weld things together to make new equipment and invent things for his farm. I thought he meant like robots and things, but Dad says no. Nothing in there looked like anything to do with animals, except maybe some more pieces of fence.

I decided that since Mom and Dad are busy, I should start trying to clean some things up around here. Don't worry, I got out my work gloves and my safety goggles, like the first day Dad took me out to do some work with him, before he figured out he didn't know how to work any of the machinery and we didn't have money for fence posts or trellis wire. (Mom says she'll teach him how to drive the tractor when she has time, but who knows when she'll have time? She has a lot of articles on her list, and that's what pays the bills right now.)

Great-Uncle Jim left huge piles of junk all over the yard, among the big trees and behind the buildings. I thought at first I'd sort them out by type, because I like things to be orderly. But after dragging about twenty tires through the dirt, I gave up on that. (How did Great-Uncle Jim get that many tires, anyway? Maybe he had friends that snuck their junk in his piles too?

I bet he never even noticed. But why was he saving half a refrigerator door and five rusty stop signs? I don't think you're supposed to take those home, even if they're lying on the sidewalk.)

So I took a big long stick and started poking the piles, watching out for the loose lengths of rusty barbed wire that sprang out at me sometimes when stuff shifted, and looked to see what was there.

But the thing I wanted to tell you about wasn't in a pile at all. It was behind a pile. I walked around toward a big blackberry bush and found some dirty sawhorses next to a bunch of stumps. It looked like there had been a fire or something.

Next to them, lying on its side in the tall weeds, there was a little house, with a front door that opened and closed. It looked like it was for those very small dogs that ride around in purses. (Do you ever wonder if those purses are full of poop? I do.)

It was a little creepy, all abandoned like that, and when the blackberry bush rustled, I ran back toward the barn and decided that was enough exploring. I felt even lonelier too.

Sorry, Abuelita, I didn't mean to mope. I am healthy and well and have plenty to eat. I just miss you.

Te quiero,
Soficita

PS Dad says some things called crawdads that look like lobsters live in the creek. Maybe I won't go wading tomorrow.

PPS I just saw a boy ride down the street on a bicycle. He looked like he might be my age. I wonder if he's riding home from the library. Or maybe there's somewhere else around here that kids like to go.

PPPS Mom put me in charge of typing next week's to-do lists. See? We are all very busy with important things. I don't know why I felt a little sad tonight.

MOM'S TO-DO'S:

Write "25 Ways to Tell Your Family You Love Them from Far Away" (due 6/11)

Write "10 Things That Make a New House Feel Like Home" (due 6/11)

Write "How to Tell Your Kids You're Moving" (due 6/12)

Write "50 Tips to Save Money on a Big Move" (due 6/12)

Write "Car Checklist: Check These Key Things Before That Big Trip" (due 6/13)

Write "How to Survive in a Small Town: A Guide for Former City Dwellers" (due 6/13)

Pitch articles for next week

Work on the mystery novel, if there's time

SOPHIE'S TO-DO'S:

Read at least one book this week

Help cook dinner

Dry dishes

Clean the part of the attic that's mine

Take out trash, recycling & compost

Sort out some of Great-Uncle Jim's junk

Remind Dad to take library books back

DAD'S TO-DO'S:

Fill out job applications for at least three grocery stores

Do résumé training at the office of unemployment

Try to find out who to talk to about how to renovate a farm

Talk to the bank about a loan???

Cook dinner

Wash dishes

Clean bathroom & kitchen

SOPHIE, WHERE ARE MY READING GLASSES?
To Do ~ Mom
DAD TO DO:
SOPHIE
Sophie's To do:

Blackbird Farm

June 11, 2014

Mariposa García González
Somewhere Gregory can't deliver the mail to

Querida Abuelita,

I told you I found a little house. This morning, I woke
up really early, like farmers do in cartoons. (Dad isn't
that kind of farmer yet. Mom says she has no intention
of ever being a farmer, even though she knows how to
drive a tractor and prune grapes and everything. She
had enough of working on a farm when she was younger.
She and Dad have a deal where she's pretending she's
on a rural writer's retreat and getting her writing work
done. She says I don't have to be a farmer either. But if
I'm going to live on a farm, I guess I might as well be a
farmer.) Anyway, I was still wondering about that house.
This might seem a little strange to you, but I wanted to
make sure I didn't just dream about it. That it was really
real. And maybe I could start getting things set up like
they used to be, just in case we could make this into a
farm with animals again.

So I went outside, before I had breakfast or anything,
back by those stumps I was talking about. And the little

house was right where I remembered it. And a little white chicken was standing in front of it, glaring at it, first with one eye and then with the other.

She looked at me. (I think she was a girl chicken? She didn't crow.) She looked pretty mad. Also, she looked like the right size for the house.

It's about as long as I am tall, but I dragged it out of the bushes eventually and got it upright. My arms got pretty scratched up, and I didn't have my gloves, but it's okay; we all got tetanus shots before Dad's insurance ran out.

The chicken looked at it, and then she looked at me. Then she started pecking at the ground.

I thought she was probably hungry. I didn't want to leave her there all by herself, but I didn't know what else to do. When I stepped closer, she hopped away, only a few steps, but fast; I wasn't going to catch her like that.

So I ran back to the house, and very quietly got some wilted lettuce and an apple. They seemed like something a chicken might eat. And I filled up one of Great-Uncle Jim's ten thousand jam jars with water. No one will miss that. Then I very quietly went outside again, and ran back.

I couldn't see the chicken anywhere at first. I was nervous for her, and sad for me. Then I saw the blackberry bushes shake, and my heart about stopped for a moment, and all my muscles got ready to run. I thought maybe it was that black thing; maybe Mom was wrong and it was a wolf or a very small bear or something dangerous. But then I saw it was just the little white chicken, scratching around.

I put the lettuce and the apple down with the jar of water, near the little house. I didn't try to catch her or touch her. She held very still while I put them down. She didn't try to peck me. When I took a few steps away, she rushed at the food, so I guess she was hungry. She kept looking around, though, so I wonder if she was lonely.

I didn't tell my parents. Not yet.

I think I'm going to draw a picture of her for you. That way, if I can't keep her, I'll have something to remember her by.

Te extraño,
Soficita

June 11, 2014

Mr. James Brown

Valhalla, maybe? (I asked Dad where you would be now,
since you're dead, and he thought about it for a while.
Then he told me about Valhalla, because he said your
great-granddad was Norwegian, but he doesn't know if
you believed in that stuff or not.)

Dear Great-Uncle Jim,

Did you have a small white angry chicken? I hope so.
Maybe I could keep her if she was yours. Did she have
a name? I hear you had lots of animals while you were
alive. Is that why you had a barn? What happened to
them? I like your barn.

Dad says he brought me here to visit when I was
really young. I wish I remembered, but I don't. I'm sorry.
And I'm really sorry you died before I came back. Dad
feels really bad about that too, especially since you left
us your farm. Gregory says you were a good guy, always
inventing things. I bet he'd tell me to say hi if he knew I
was writing to you.

Love,
Sophie

PS What were you saving all those piles of junk for? Inventions?

PPS What am I supposed to do with this chicken now?

PPPS Don't come back from the dead to answer, okay? I'll figure it out somehow.

June 11, 2014 (later)

Mariposa García González

Mictlan (I asked Mom if there was anywhere like Valhalla in Mexico. She said maybe Mictlan, where dead people do everyday stuff except for on El Día de los Muertos, the Day of the Dead, when they go see their families. Mom says maybe if you were in Mictlan you could read my letter. [Mom had a calavera with a typewriter, so maybe you could even type back.] I know you are a good Catholic, but maybe you could go to Mictlan for a visit? Like for a field trip? I wish I could really tell you all this.)

Querida Abuelita,

Here are some pictures of my chicken for you.

Isn't she beautiful? I think I'm going to name her Henrietta. Did you ever read The Hoboken Chicken Emergency? It's about a 266-pound chicken named Henrietta. This Henrietta is short, even for a chicken, I think, but that's why it's funny. We hung out for most of the afternoon. So far, she likes to chase bugs and peck at everything except me.

After I finished dinner and dried the dishes that Dad washed, I went out to check on her. It was dark and windy and kind of spooky, the way pumpkin patches are at the end of October. Haunted-farm spooky. But I thought the chicken might be nervous too. I mean, she's probably been through a lot, living on her own in the blackberry bushes.

I wish there weren't so many huge junk piles for things to hide behind, or all that rustling dead grass, or the weird twisted trees. I guess you don't have streetlights in the middle of farms, but maybe I should save up for a bigger flashlight. LA is never this dark. It didn't help my nerves that I saw right away that the little house's door was shut with the bolt latched, and I know for sure I left the door wide open in case the chicken wanted to go inside.

I stood there for a while, feeling creeped out all over. The hair on the back of my neck stood up and the wind was snaking all around and the weird nature sounds made me wonder what else was nearby. I know, I shouldn't read so many scary books. But I really, really didn't want to open that door. I really, really didn't want whatever had shut that door to see me out there. But what if it had locked my chicken out of her house? How would she feel, locked out all night? What if she thought it was me who locked her out, or me who didn't let her in?

I stood there and looked hard at all the bushes and trees and junk and everything, to make sure nothing moved. But I didn't even see Henrietta. I shined my flashlight all around, and the glass jam jar of water caught the light and startled me. I didn't see any glowing eyes, but there were no white feathers, either.

I made myself walk across the grass to the little house and unlatch the door. I know I held my breath while I opened it. But when I looked, Henrietta was inside, perched on a branch. She opened one eye and looked mad. So I turned and ran all the way back to the house and locked our front door. I think you'd agree that was only sensible.

When Dad came to tuck me in, I wondered if he would say anything about the chicken. But he didn't. I don't think it was him that latched the door.

I know I have to tell them. I just wanted to pretend for a little while that I could have a chicken. But I think maybe I waited too long. I think it's going to be harder now to give her up.

Te extraño mucho,
Soficita

Blackbird Farm

June 12, 2014

Mr. or Ms. Catalog People
Redwood Farm Supply
Gravenstein, CA 95472

Dear People Who Sell Special Chickens,

Look, maybe Mom was right about not writing while I
was angry. I'm really sorry I said that stuff. Probably
you've been busy too. But now I really need you to write
back, even if you don't send me a catalog. Because a
chicken showed up yesterday, and I think it must be one
of yours, because it is really definitely not an ordinary
chicken. I'm pretty sure my parents are going to freak
out, and I really need to figure out what to do. What are
you supposed to do with a found chicken—is it like a
found dog? Do chickens go to the pound? But it's got to
be yours. It's really unusual, for sure. Can you please
come get it quickly?

Sincerely,
Sophie

PS Don't worry, I'm going to the library now and I'm sure
they'll have a book on how to take care of chickens. And

I'm not stupid. I won't tell them mine is special.

PPS It's small and white and looks mad. And it's pretty loud, which is another problem.

Blackbird Farm

June 12, 2014

Mr. James Brown
Who knows?

Dear Great-Uncle Jim,

You know that chicken I told you about? It can use the Force.

I would worry that you wouldn't believe me, but I think it used to be yours, so you must know already. Besides, you're dead.

First of all, the little chicken house wasn't where I left it last night. It's up on four stumps now, and it's stuck on tight. I thought Dad moved it (Mom's working—she hasn't been outside in days), and that worried me, because I haven't told them a chicken showed up yet. But then I remembered he'd gone to town right after breakfast.

Then I realized the door was shut and latched, and I know I unlatched it and left it open last night. That didn't make me very happy. I started looking around for Henrietta, and when I came back around the big junk pile, the door was open.

I almost started running then. Only dumb kids in movies wait around for evil strangers to pick them off.

But what about Henrietta? (That's what I'm calling her. Hope that's okay.) I couldn't leave her behind if there was stranger danger around.

There was a noise from in the little house, kind of a thump, and I froze. Henrietta stuck her head out the door and hopped down on the ground, bawking and cackling and having a huge old chicken conversation. I tried to shush her as quietly as I could, and kept my eyes wide open so I could try and grab her if anything moved at all. She walked over to her jam jar and glared at me and bawked some more.

And then I guess she got tired of asking nicely. She got real quiet, so I stared at her. And then she glared at the jam jar—which, I suddenly realized, had tipped over so there was no more water for her to drink—and . . . Well, I'm just going to say it. The jam jar floated off the ground, sailed over, and landed at my feet.

As soon as it landed, she squawked and went back to pecking at the dandelions in the blackberry bushes.

I don't know what I was thinking, but when Henrietta looked up and glared at me, I grabbed the jam jar and ran for the hose. After I filled it up, I stared at it for a while, in case it was a magic jam jar. But I couldn't make it move at all.

I guess I might as well tell you I was kind of afraid to go back. I've read a lot of books about kids who find magic stuff. A lot of scary things happen to them. And

I don't even know how to take care of regular chickens yet, let alone chickens with superpowers. I might have freaked out for a bit, and I wrote to that company you probably got her from. I told them to come get her.

But I couldn't leave her out there without any water or anything. Gregory's fast, but the mail is still slow. I got another apple and picked up the jam jar again (I put my gloves on first this time, just in case) and I took them back by the little house.

Henrietta wasn't hurting anything, or even floating anything. She was just scratching in the dirt with her big old scaly dinosaur feet and pouncing on bugs. She didn't even look mad. I gave her the apple and the water and she had a drink. Chickens look really funny when they drink, like people gargling.

I know I'm not a hero. I just moved to a farm, and I wanted to have chickens. But, you know what? There are books about kids like me, too. Sometimes they're boring, but sometimes they're not. And sometimes they're sad at the end, especially the ones with animals. But not always.

I'm going to write back to that company and tell them never mind, I'll keep her. Then I'll tell Mom and Dad. Only, not about the superpowers.

I have to go now—I think I see Gregory coming up the street.

Love,

Sophie

PS I wish you could tell me if you have any tips. I'm pretty sure the library won't have any books on what to do next.

Redwood Farm

send to sophie at jim's farm

sssxxxxsophie,

sounds like one of jims, xthat he got from me.
tell me what happened//x. don't llet antyowne
take her.,. oorrgive her to anyowne 777and don't
tell anyone. no matter what,.,..
   sorry xxtyxpewriter is broken.

                              agnes

p.s. be very careful;ll.

Agnes
Redwood Farm Supply
Gravenstein, CA 95472

Dear Agnes,

Sorry to hear about your typewriter. It's fine with me if you want to write by hand. Maybe you should print, though, so I can read it? My grandmother's cursive was terrible—no one could read it, so we can't make any of her recipes now. (She's dead.)

So here's what happened. A little white chicken came out of the blackberry bushes out behind the barn on Great-Uncle Jim's farm the other day. She made a jam jar and maybe a little chicken house float. And she can open and shut and even latch the door by herself. She hasn't done anything else yet. Is she going to?

If she was Great-Uncle Jim's, I think I should keep her. I'm very responsible. Do you have a manual or something? On special chickens, I mean? I already got a library book on how to take care of regular chickens.

Sincerely,
Sophie

PS She looks lonely. What happened to Great-Uncle Jim's other chickens?

PPS There's a metal garbage can in the barn that's about a quarter full of seeds and mashed-up dried stuff. It says LAYER CRUMBLE on the lid in big black letters. Is that chicken food?

PPPS I saw something black run really fast down the road today. Do you know what it was? Is it dangerous to chickens?

PPPPS What exactly am I supposed to be very careful of? The chicken? Or the black thing? Or something else?

Bantam White Leghorn

Diminutive height, white plumage, yellow featherless legs and feet. Small red single comb, white
earlobes.

Small white eggs, frequent layer. Easily able
to stand up to standard-sized chickens in mixed
flocks. It is not uncommon for this breed of bantam to be the top of the pecking order among
milder-mannered breeds.

June 14, 2014
(later, but I have to wait until
tomorrow to mail this because
Gregory already came today)

Agnes
Redwood Farm Supply
Gravenstein, CA 95472

Dear Agnes,

Someone tried to steal Henrietta! A white lady, about my
parents' age. Dad said she said her name was Sue.
      She didn't get her, though.

                    Sincerely,
                    Sophie

PS Is she going to try again? How am I supposed
to protect Henrietta when I go to the library or the
grocery store?

Mr. James Brown
Wherever you are now

Dear Great-Uncle Jim,

Sorry I thought your farm was boring before. I didn't
know there were going to be chicken thieves.

Agnes from the chicken company wrote me a scary
letter earlier, so I decided I'd better get prepared, just in
case. Good thing I did.

The chicken book I read said that if you want to get
your chickens back in the henhouse at night, you can
throw some treats inside and train them to go after
them. It said they like sunflower seeds, and you sure
have a lot of those in that trash can in the barn. (Why
did you keep things in trash cans that weren't trash,
and keep your junk in big piles? Someone could get
confused.) So I put some seeds in a jar, one of those blue
ones with an old metal lid, and I put the lid on tight so
no squirrels would eat them. I put the jar back by the
henhouse. Henrietta looked at it, but she didn't float it
or anything. The jar was a little dusty, but I think it's
okay—after all, she pecks around in the dirt all day, and

that book said she even eats small rocks. To grind things up with, in her gizzard. See? This is educational. If you weren't dead, I'd have you tell Mom and Dad.

Then I put my gloves on and dug around on your workbench until I found an old padlock, hanging open on a hook. No matter how hard I looked, I couldn't find the key, though. Maybe you should have put it on the same hook. Anyway, I took the padlock out and hung it on the chicken coop latch, next to the open door. Just in case.

Chickens are really funny, and I like your chicken a whole lot, now that I'm used to her, but they aren't very huggable. So I just watched her for a little bit while she scratched up all the dirt with her toes and put her eyeball right down near the ground to check and see if anything wiggled. I swallowed a few times when I felt sad. Then I walked up to the house.

When I got there, a beat-up orange pickup was parked in the driveway with a dog crate in the back, and I heard some woman's voice inside with my parents.

I knew it was probably nothing, just some visitor, but that Agnes had made me nervous. I turned and ran back the way I'd come. Just in case.

Henrietta saw me coming, and when I threw some sunflower seeds into the chicken house, she flapped up and went in after them. I shoved her water jar inside too. I shut the door, latched it, put the lock through the hole, and locked it.

Henrietta didn't like that one bit. She started squawking. The latch rattled, and then the padlock started banging against the latch.

"Hush, silly chicken," I told her. "Agnes said someone might try to take you, and someone's here now. Be quiet, like you aren't even there."

But I guess she doesn't understand me, because she just kept making a racket. Or else she was too mad at me to care.

I was feeling sick to my stomach. I couldn't stay out there, but I didn't want to talk to my parents or the stranger, either. I'm not a very good liar, and my mom is really, really good at telling when people aren't telling the truth. So I went to the barn. I like it there, and I could see if anyone headed for the henhouse.

I was separating screws from nails into jars on your workbench when they came up the path. I about fainted when I heard voices. But I kept working; I didn't want to look suspicious.

Dad stuck his head through the door. "Soph, you haven't seen any chickens, have you?"

I tried to look confused. "Around here?" I saw Mom through the doorway. Her eyes narrowed. My stomach felt even worse.

But she didn't say anything.

The woman behind her didn't look like a chicken thief. She was taller than my mom, and really thin, like those people who go to yoga twice a day and don't eat real food anymore. She had brown hair and a tan— almost as dark as me—and she was wearing jeans and a T-shirt. She smiled when she saw me, and it wasn't a scary smile, like the ones in movies I'm not supposed to be old enough to watch.

I smiled back.

"Sorry to bother you," she said. "Some of my chickens got out, and I'm having trouble rounding them up."

Maybe her chickens really did get out. Maybe I was just nervous. Or maybe Henrietta really did belong to her. But Agnes told me not to give Henrietta to anyone. And Henrietta was not just a regular chicken. "No problem," I said. "Is your farm around here?"

Mom looked back at the woman. "I'm sorry, I didn't even ask if you were a neighbor—but of course you must be. Which farm is yours?"

The woman hesitated, and I saw Mom's eyes narrow again. (I told you she was good at this.) "Briar Farm is mine, over by the lake. Mostly vegetables and poultry."

Dad looked surprised. "That's a couple miles, isn't it?"

Mom shook her head. "I'm sorry about your chickens, but they must be dog food or roadkill by now. How could they have made it this far?" She started to turn back up the path.

The woman frowned. "I know it's a long shot, but I'd like to look around, just in case."

"Sure," Dad said before I could say anything. "Good luck finding them. What kind did you say they were?"

The woman was already hurrying down the path toward the henhouse. "Mixed flock—all kinds," she called back.

Mom was still frowning, looking at me, but when Dad headed for the house, she followed.

I watched the lady go, and bit my lip until it got all bloody. Then I thought I heard a squawk, and I started running after her.

It was a good thing I did, because even though Henrietta was silent when I got there, that lady was holding a screwdriver on top of the padlock and hitting it with a hammer.

"Stop!" I screamed.

She looked back at me, but she didn't stop.

I didn't know what else to do. So I got out my whistle, the one my mom insists I wear everywhere, and I gathered every bit of breath I had left after running and screaming, and I blew that thing.

It was a loud one, too. I blew it again and again, just in case the wind was blowing funny or something.

That surprised her. She hit the screwdriver at a weird angle, and it flew into the bushes. She glared at me, and took off running, the long way that isn't really a path, around the barn. I think she's been here before.

I didn't want to leave Henrietta, so I didn't run after

her. I was just standing there when Dad ran into the clearing and grabbed me so hard he almost knocked me over.

"Are you okay?" he shouted.

"Yes, Dad, I'm fine. That lady was breaking and entering," I explained.

Dad stared at me. "That whistle is for emergencies only!" he shouted.

"Dad, I know. This was an emergency. That lady was bad news."

Dad grabbed my hand and started running back down the path toward the house, so I ran too.

After I explained to Mom that the lady had a hammer and screwdriver, I guess in her purse, and after I told Dad I was fine about sixty more times, and after Mom called 911 back and told them her daughter was fine and not to send anyone after all (even though I explained this was a police emergency and she should have them come see), and after I'd had about ten lectures on how the whistle was Only For Emergencies, and I'd probably Just Taken Twenty Years Off Their Lives, and Mom had finally explained to Dad that the point was not to terrify me into never using the whistle again, I asked them to come back with me to the henhouse. It was getting dark, and I hoped Henrietta had calmed down and was going to sleep. And I needed them to believe me about that lady, in case she came back.

The henhouse was locked up tight, totally silent.

Mom found the screwdriver in the bushes. Dad wouldn't help look for it. "Hammer marks on the end, sure enough," she said.

"Like all screwdrivers," Dad said. But he did look at it.

Mom put her arm around my shoulders. "Good work, Soficita. I wonder what she wanted with that old thing, though. I can't even remember seeing it before." She studied the henhouse.

Dad snorted. "It's been here all along—it just blends in with the rest of Uncle Jim's junk." (Sorry about that—I hope he didn't hurt your feelings.)

I know I probably should have told them about Henrietta then. But as long as she kept quiet, I wanted to keep her a secret a little longer. At least long enough to make sure they knew that lady was a thief, so they wouldn't give Henrietta to her.

I shrugged. "The lady went that way. It looked like she knew her way around."

Dad looked at the path along the fence, where I pointed. He frowned. "Maybe she's been hiding stuff on Uncle Jim's property."

"Why would she hide her stuff here?" I asked.

Dad shrugged. "Anything she doesn't want found on her property—drugs, or stolen goods. Good thing I ran her off, then."

I won't bother to tell you the rest of that conversation. It had nothing to do with the chicken. But I don't think they'll be happy to see that lady again.

I'll figure out the rest tomorrow, I guess.

Love,
Sophie

June 14, 2014

Mariposa García González
Somewhere wonderful, I hope

Querida Abuelita,

I don't know if you read the letters I wrote to Great-Uncle
Jim or not, or if he told you what's been going on here
(if you're in the same place), but I've been pretty busy
lately. (Sorry to write to him first, but it seemed like he'd
want to know what was going on with his chicken. His
letters are in the wooden box on my desk here too, if you
need to catch up on what's been happening.) And today?
Today . . . Well, I was really scared. But I think things
are okay now. So if you're out there somewhere, looking
out for me, like you always said you always would, thank
you.

    I hope that lady never comes back.

    I hope Mom and Dad aren't too mad. I know I have to
tell them about Henrietta.

Te quiero,

Soficita

PS I was talking to Gregory, our mailman, yesterday about how I write you letters sometimes because I miss you. He said he misses his grandmothers too. He told me that some people send messages to their dead families by burning their letters (very carefully, and not inside barns—he was very clear about that), or putting them in a special place on a special day. He didn't know of any ways for the dead to send letters back. But, when I asked if there could be ways he didn't know about, he said, "There are more things in heaven and earth, Sophie Brown, than are dreamt of in our philosophies." Mom laughed when I told her and said Gregory knows his Shakespeare. But I liked the way it sounded. Gregory has a deep voice, and he kind of boomed it out, not yelling, but strong. It wasn't scary, but it still gave me goose bumps.

PPS I still wish you could write to me, though.

Blackbird Farm

Mr. James Brown
Wherever you are now

Dear Great-Uncle Jim,

When I went out to the henhouse this morning, the padlock was rattling and rattling, and Henrietta was squawking her head off. Good thing I get up early now.

It was pretty obvious that Henrietta doesn't know how to open padlocks on her own. So I went to borrow some of your tools from the barn.

I sort of put the tip of the screwdriver where the loop went into the lock, and then hit the end of the screwdriver with the hammer. The screwdriver slipped, and I hit my thumb really hard and the lock stayed locked. I did this more times than I'd like to tell you about. Maybe that lady had been watching too much TV, and only thought she had a good plan.

Meanwhile, Henrietta was still freaking out, and I couldn't blame her because she probably didn't have any food or water left, and my parents were going to be mad if I wasn't at breakfast.

My mom always says when things are really bad, stop

and think your hardest, because most people don't think at all under those circumstances and then they make things worse. So I tried. I walked all the way around the henhouse before I noticed something important.

Turns out, it's easier to unscrew door hinges than it is to break locks. It's quiet, and it goes pretty fast, even if you have the wrong size screwdriver. You might have to unscrew the latch too, and wiggle everything a lot, but you can probably make it work.

Henrietta stuck her head out the door as soon as I got it off. She gave me a hard look, first with one eye and then with the other, and fluffed out her feathers. Then she hopped down on the ground, turned her back on me, and started scratching up the dirt. Once she got busy with that, she stopped squawking and started making her little chortling noises again. I think she's fine now.

I'll let you know what my parents say. Right now, I have to go—I promised Dad I'd make him breakfast for Father's Day. All we have is oatmeal, but I will make him a smiley face with brown sugar. He likes that. Someday, maybe I can cook him some eggs from my own chicken.

Love,
Sophie

ReDWOOD Farm

xxxxxxxxxxxxxxxxxsory broken

dear sophie,

Xxxxxhenrietta is a bantam white legxxhorn.
you know why shes unusual. Yes feed her layer
crumble seeds etc. gather xeggs every day
777a7nd rrefrigerate for at least a week -no
chicks. do keep her safe. look out for jims 6
other chickensn. don't put normal chickens
with her, and no roosters. catch the black one
too x-cochinxx.

                              agnes

- please send with beginning poultry course
pt 1- file cabinet - top drawer. -

ARE CHICKENS RIGHT FOR YOU?

PLEASE CHOOSE THE ANSWER THAT BEST FITS YOUR RESPONSE FOR EACH QUESTION. YOU MUST ANSWER ALL QUESTIONS IN ORDER TO SCORE THE QUIZ EFFECTIVELY.

1. Are you afraid of birds?
   A) Certainly not! Is anyone? I don't believe it.
   B) Maybe a little bit, but my chickens would never know it.
✓ C) Yes, but only mean geese (and large raptors after I watch Hitchcock movies late at night).
   D) Yes, I run and hide whenever a robin flies over my yard.

2. Are you afraid of bugs?
   A) No, I eat them when someone dares me.
   B) No, but they're gross and I would never touch one.
✓ C) Yes, but only the bugs that bite or sting me.
   D) Yes, I have a huge can of bug-killer spray and replace it often.

3. If you had the flu, what would you do?
   A) Go check on the chickens in the morning and evening, and clean out the coop while I'm at it, and only then collapse back into bed.
✓ B) Ask a family member or friend to tend to the chickens' basic daily needs.
   C) Oversleep, then remember the chickens and rush outside to check on them.
   D) Forget I have chickens; I'm too busy vomiting.

4. If you were going on vacation, what would you do?

   A) I would never go on vacation again if I had chickens.

✓ B) Ask a neighbor or friend to stop by to let the chickens in and out of the henhouse and check on their food and water.

   C) Install an automatic door and put two weeks' worth of food and water in the coop.

   D) Just go on vacation; chickens can take care of themselves; they should be fine for two weeks.

5. When was the last time you took care of an animal?

   A) I have always cared for at least 200 chickens, and have never forgotten anything for any of them; they are immortal due to my perfect care.

   B) I had a cat that needed food and water every day, and I took care of it until it died of old age.

   C) I had a dog that needed food, water, and a walk every day; my mom did all that.

   D) I had a goldfish. I forgot about it five minutes after we got home. That was five years ago. (I wonder if it's still there.)

✓ E) I never had a pet before. We lived in an apartment.

6. Why do you want chickens?

   A) They're so cute and fluffy and soft and cuddly.

✓ B) For the eggs.

   C) My family is allergic to dogs and cats and goldfish.

   D) So I can chop their heads off with an ax and watch them run around the barnyard as they die; that sounds like the most fun I've had in a long time.

7. How often do you eat eggs?

   A) At every meal. I crack them and slurp them down raw out of the shell.

✓ B) Pretty often; my family bakes and likes eggs for breakfast on the weekend.

C) Sometimes, and I have friends and family to share them with.

D) Is that what they're for? Are you sure they're not poisonous?

8. **If you accidentally stepped in a pile of chicken droppings while collecting eggs one morning, what would you do?**

A) Take off my shoe and carefully carry it over to tip into the compost bin, not wasting a bit of the precious excrement fertilizer.

✓ B) Wipe it off on some nearby grass or hay and go about my business.

C) Have to go inside and wash my shoe before doing anything else.

D) Eeeeww! That would be so disgusting, I could never, ever wear that shoe again in my entire life.

9. **Which answer best describes your background with chickens?**

A) I am a twelfth-generation chicken farmer and lay eggs myself every morning; you could say I'm one with my chickens.

B) I have met a few chickens, and I think they're the neatest birds ever (except maybe penguins, or owls).

✓ C) I read an article about them once and thought they might be fun.

D) I have eaten chicken nuggets once in a while.

10. **Why are you taking this class?**

A) I know everything already and would like to tell you all the things you're teaching wrong.

✓ B) I am learning all I can about chickens from books, farmers, and classes like yours.

   C) I was bored, and it was cheap.

   D) My parent/teacher/employer is forcing me to take this class.

HOW TO SCORE YOUR QUIZ:

Questions 1–9:
Give yourself:
1 point for each A
3 points for each B
2 points for each C
0 points for each D
2 *points for each E*

Question 10:
Give yourself:
10 points for A
30 points for B
20 points for C
0 points for D

MATCH YOUR TOTAL POINTS TO THE SCORE RANGE BELOW.

39+ points: Almost Ready for Chicks

Congratulations! You're realistic about the responsibilities and what you'll need to learn. You like chickens and deserve some of your own. You'll do your best to take care of them. Please continue with Lesson 1.

20–38 points: Just Bored

I'm sorry you're bored, but please find a hobby that does not involve living things, or learn more about why you'd actually want chickens before you acquire your own. With your current score, you aren't eligible to purchase chicks from Redwood Farm Supply. From here, you have two options:

1. Send in this quiz for a full refund, and go get yourself a library card instead. Or,

2. You may continue your lessons. After learning more about

chickens and completing Lessons 1 and 2, you may wish to retake the quiz or write a 1,000-word essay on why you ought to be able to keep chickens. These submissions will be seriously reviewed and your status may change, so do not give up hope.

9–19 points: Poultry Know-It-All

I'm sure you're a very good chicken keeper, but you must agree there's no point in your continuing to take this class. Please send in this quiz for a full refund for any chickens or chicken supplies you may have ordered; your lessons are at an end. I suggest you take that money and save it for your advanced-degree program in agriculture, where you can tell internationally renowned scholars they're doing it all wrong. Doesn't that sound nicer?

0 points: Mad, Bad, and Dangerous to Chickens

You don't want to take this class and are certainly not eligible to purchase chickens from Redwood Farm Supply. Please give this attached note to your parent/teacher/employer:

> Regretfully, Redwood Farm Supply has encountered an error which cannot be rectified, and we can no longer ship lessons to this student. May we suggest this student pursue a career with nonliving things in place of a career in poultry.

If you are concerned about this score, we suggest you seek professional help regarding that ax issue and perhaps develop your level of responsibility, beginning with a single bean plant. Do not proceed with other organisms until you can successfully grow the bean plant. Best wishes.

BEGINNER'S CORRESPONDENCE COURSE
IN PROPER CARE AND HOUSING FOR POULTRY:
CHICKEN EDITION

Lesson 1: Nutritional Needs and Other Considerations

Feed: Like all animals, chickens have complex dietary requirements that must be met if they are to remain healthy and lay well. Luckily for you, Redwood Farm Supply has invested decades of research in developing feed that meets your birds' needs perfectly; you must choose the correct type to purchase.

Laying hens:	Redwood Farm Supply Layer Crumble	17% protein content, sufficient calcium for daily egg production
Pullets, roosters & mixed-age flocks:	Redwood Farm Supply Starter Crumble + crushed oyster shells	19% protein, avoids kidney damage to younger birds
Chicks:	Redwood Farm Supply Chick Feed	19% protein, medicated against coccidiosis

(Note: Contact us if seeking organic farm certification)

Remember, even chickens who can forage for insects and other foods will get the majority of their nutritional needs from this feed, so choose wisely.

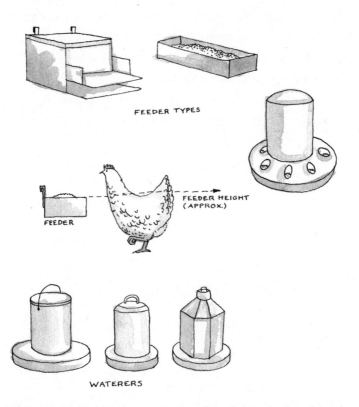

FEEDER TYPES

FEEDER HEIGHT
(APPROX.)

FEEDER

WATERERS

Feeders: Raise the feeder to the height of the chickens' backs, and avoid locating it under a roost or branch. Chickens will defecate in their own food if the feeder is lower. Consider adding a bit of food-grade diatomaceous earth (the fossilized remains of diatoms) to the feed to reduce flies and kill internal parasites.

Water: Chickens must have access to fresh water at all times. They dehydrate dangerously quickly without it, even in cooler seasons. Check your chickens' water at least once per day. If you experience freezing temperatures in winter, check your chickens' water more frequently, breaking up ice or refilling with warm water as needed.

Grit: As chickens do not have teeth, they eat sand and small stones to fill their gizzards. When they swallow food, it is sent to the gizzard, where the grinding stones pulverize the food. If your chickens range outside, they will likely find sufficient grit on their own. If they are kept primarily inside a barn, you should provide a container of grit for them to eat as needed.

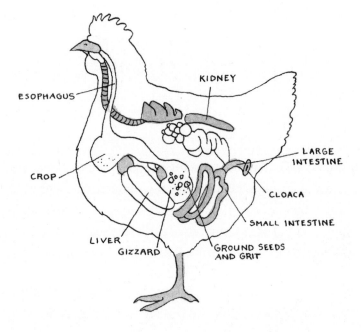

Scratch, scraps, and other treats: Chickens do not require treats, but they certainly enjoy them. Favorites include cracked corn, black oil sunflower seeds, and mealworms. You can also collect garden pests such as slugs and cutworms for your chickens, or supplement your chickens' feed with kitchen scraps such as vegetables, leftover low-fat and sugar-free dairy products, and even unspoiled cooked meats (chickens are omnivores).

OK:

CORN
SUNFLOWER SEEDS
MEALWORMS
VEGETABLE SCRAPS
LOWFAT DAIRY
UNSPOILED MEATS

What not to feed chickens: Avoid desserts, citrus peels, coffee grounds, moldy food, and junk food, and limit scraps to a small portion of your chickens' meals. Strong-smelling foods such as onions, fish, and herbs should also be avoided, as they may flavor your chickens' eggs.

AVOID:

DESSERT
CITRUS PEEL
COFFEE GROUNDS
MOLDY FOOD + CANDY
ONION
FISH
HERBS

Name: _____

CALCULATE HOW LONG A 50-POUND BAG OF FEED
WILL LAST YOUR FLOCK:

I have _____ chickens.

Each adult chicken will eat approximately ¼ (.25) pound of food per day.

50 pounds ÷ _____ chickens = _____ pounds per chicken

_____ pounds per chicken ÷ 0.25 pound per day = _____ days before I'll need more feed

CALCULATE HOW LONG A 4-GALLON (64-CUP) WATERER
WILL LAST YOUR FLOCK:

I have _____ chickens.

Each adult chicken will drink approximately 2 cups of water per day.

64 cups ÷ _____ chickens = _____ cups per chicken

_____ cups per chicken ÷ 2 cups per day = _____ days before I'll need to refill the waterer

Note: Even if your waterer should last your flock for several days, you must still check it, in case the water has been dirtied, spilled, etc.

Please submit your completed worksheet to your instructor in the envelope provided. Your results will be sent along with Lesson 2 and any supplemental materials.

June 17, 2014

Mariposa García González
Land of the Dead

Querida Abuelita,

I'm really sorry you're dead. But I bet now you can
believe in anything. And you are a good listener too.
And I don't think I need to worry Great-Uncle Jim with
all this.

This morning, I got up early, earlier than anyone
else, and I went to check on Henrietta. I dumped out her
old water and got her some new water, and gave her some
of that layer crumble in a little plastic tub, with a few
sunflower seeds, because I know she loves them. I looked
in the nest boxes, but there weren't any eggs in there
(and no chicken poop either, thank goodness).

Then I put my gloves on and got a trowel and kind of
scraped the chicken poop off the floor of the henhouse
into a bucket and dumped it in the blackberry bushes.
(I don't think anything could hurt those bushes.) It
was smelly and gross, but no way was I going to make
Henrietta sleep in there with it. I found some straw in
a corner of the barn, all tied together with wire into a

block, and I pulled some of it out and put it in the nest boxes and on the floor of the henhouse. My library book says you can just take out the part that the chicken poop is on and replace that when you need to. I bet the first person to figure that out was really happy about it.

Then, when I knew Henrietta was all set for the day, and I had tidied up the edge of the junk pile so she wouldn't trip over it, and found some dandelions in a different part of the yard and picked them for her, since she really likes them, and when I had drawn one last picture of her, I left her there and went inside to talk to my parents about her.

I really, really tried. But when my parents found out there was a small white chicken back by the old henhouse, they insisted on calling the lady who'd come looking for her chickens, to see if it was hers.

I reminded them she'd tried to break into the henhouse. I told them this was probably Great-Uncle Jim's chicken. I even took them out to meet Henrietta (crossing my fingers that her water jar wasn't empty or anything like that).

But Mom wanted to know how I'd feel if I was searching for my chickens and someone else had them.

I'd feel terrible. But Agnes told me not to give Henrietta away, and not to tell anyone she's unusual. And I sure didn't want a thief to use Henrietta's powers for evil purposes. I had to find a way to keep her.

But Mom talked about what the neighbors would think if they found out we'd had someone else's livestock and hadn't given it back right away, and I knew I'd lost, because you know how Mom is about not being seen as one of those problem people. You guys must have had a hard time when you were young, Abuelita, because even though Mom was born here and speaks perfect English, she says you have to be twice as honest and neighborly when everyone assumes you're an undocumented immigrant, and she won't have me growing up with problems like that. What was it like, really, Abuelita? I know about ICE, and I know they can't take citizens like me and Mom away, so you won't scare me. Too bad I never asked you before. Mom won't tell me till I'm older.

But we were talking about the chicken, and about Mom making up her mind.

The only luck I had was that the lady hadn't given my parents her phone number or email address or anything. So Mom decided Dad and I should go into town to the library to look up the lady's number, while she got some work done for once. Mom's been having a rough time with this week's articles, what with all these interruptions.

Dad and I were both quiet as we drove into town. I was trying to figure out what I was going to do with Henrietta. Hide her, like Anne Frank, maybe in the barn? But Anne Frank knew to stay quiet and hide, and she still got caught.

I think Dad felt kind of guilty, because he gave my shoulders a hug when we went into the library, and said, "Buck up, Soph. There'll be other chickens eventually."

I didn't bother to answer. He really didn't understand.

Ms. O'Malley was the only one there. She spends a lot of time trying to help me find useful chicken books. (When I first got my library card and wrote Blackbird Farm on the form, she didn't know I was Dad's daughter or Jim Brown's grandniece, and she asked me how long my family was working there. I think she still feels bad about that.)

Dad and I walked up to the librarian's desk. I handed Ms. O'Malley my old library books.

Ms. O'Malley smiled hard at me. "How can I help you today, Sophie?"

My throat didn't feel like I could get any words through it, so I didn't say anything.

Dad smiled back. "It seems we need a phone number for Sue of Briar Farm, please. We found a little white chicken she lost."

Ms. O'Malley raised her eyebrows. "Sue Griegson hasn't got any bantam whites, and never has. Do you still want her phone number, or can I help you find the true owner?"

I held my breath and crossed my fingers. Can't hurt, might help, especially with magic chickens.

"She told us she had a mixed flock and some went missing. . . ." Dad frowned.

Ms. O'Malley snorted. "Sue has never raised anything but Rhode Island Reds; I swear on my honor as the vice president of our American Poultry Association chapter. You may not be a chicken person, sir, but if it isn't a big dark reddish-brown bird, it isn't Sue Griegson's."

"It's a white hen, about this big." I held up my hands to show her how big Henrietta is. Way smaller than a standard Rhode Island Red, I hoped. "She has yellow legs and a little red comb."

"Bantam White Leghorn, from the sound of it." She nodded. "The only one with bantam White Leghorns in this area was Jim Brown. Well, aside from Redwood Farm." She sighed. "When I found out Jim had died, I went over to make sure his flock was cared for, but they were nowhere to be found. There'd been storms that week, and I figured they scattered when the food ran out."

She put her hands on her hips and looked at Dad. "You inherited the farm and all its contents, right?"

Dad nodded slowly.

Ms. O'Malley smiled at me—a real smile. "Then the chicken's your responsibility. Unless you're not able to care for a single chicken?"

"Er—no, of course we can," Dad said uncomfortably. "We just wanted to make sure . . ."

"Very good, then. The poultry show will be coming up in July; there'll be a benefit auction of any unwanted birds then, if you really can't keep her. But I know your daughter's been studying poultry, so you shouldn't have any trouble," Ms. O'Malley said briskly.

Dad didn't really have anything left to say then, not even when I checked out the rest of the books on chicken care, or when I told Ms. O'Malley I was thinking about naming the chicken Henrietta, and she said that sounded suitable. (I checked out The Hoboken Chicken Emergency again, just to be sure.)

When we got back to our farm, Dad helped me cut the padlock off the door and screw the hinges back on so Henrietta could be safe in her house again. Then he helped me pull an old wooden chair out of a different junk pile and propped it up with a log so I could sit on it even though the leg was kind of broken. He hung around for a while, but I'm better at waiting than he is, and we only found one chair. So, after listening to me read the first few chapters of The Hoboken Chicken Emergency to Henrietta, to see what she thought, he went inside to explain it all to Mom. I noticed he didn't laugh at the funny parts, though.

I'll see what she thinks at dinner, I guess. I'll cross my fingers again, under the table.

Te quiero,
Soficita

PS Once I know for sure I can keep her, I'm going to see if that black streak could really be another superchicken.

PPS Did you know that chickens look really funny when they run? Kind of like a Tyrannosaurus rex combined with an airplane, if an airplane flapped its wings really hard. And squawked. I love having a chicken.

Agnes
Redwood Farm Supply
Gravenstein, CA 95472

Dear Agnes,

I told my parents about Henrietta. There were some complications while they wanted to tell that lady who tried to steal her (she said she'd lost her chickens), but Ms. O'Malley got Dad straightened out. Why didn't you tell me that lady only has Rhode Island Reds?

Anyway, it was a good thing you sent me your chicken class, because when Dad told Mom and she pointed out I didn't know anything about chickens and she didn't have time to teach me, I told them I was already signed up for your free curriculum, so I could study over the summer.

Mom is very big on education. She looked surprised but impressed when I showed her your worksheet and my chicken books from the library. She looked them over carefully, and then she told Dad that it was true that if we're going to stay, I ought to learn something about farm life.

Dad (who seems kind of depressed lately—he hasn't got a new job yet, and I think the farm's in worse shape than he expected) said there's no way we'll have money for chicken feed or supplies this year.

If we had any money left, I'd think we might be moving somewhere else soon. But don't worry, we don't have anywhere else to go. So I showed him my worksheet too, and told him about the chicken food in the metal garbage can in the barn, and said one small chicken probably doesn't eat much, but I would calculate it anyway, if he'd help me weigh the can. (No reason to bring up the black streak chicken yet.) I also pointed out that it's summer, there's nothing to do, I don't know anybody, and every kid I ever met was already going to know this stuff, so I might as well learn something before I tried going to school here. I went up to my attic room then, since I couldn't get any more words out without crying, and read my library books for a while.

Mom and Dad came up a little while later. They both gave me big hugs. They decided I could try keeping Henrietta, as long as we have chicken food, but that we just don't have enough money for extra pets right now. But don't worry, I'll find a way to earn some money for more feed, so Henrietta and the other chicken can be safe. I'll try to catch it tomorrow.

Sincerely,
Sophie

Blackbird Farm

Agnes
Redwood Farm Supply
Gravenstein, CA 95472

Dear Agnes,

I have to tell you, even though I want to be an excellent chicken keeper, I wasn't so sure this course was going to work out. I mean, I don't want it to be too easy, but when I started working on Lesson 1, I had to borrow my mom's dictionary five times just to figure out what you were talking about.

Then, once I knew what you were saying, I got worried that maybe I was feeding Henrietta all wrong. I mean, I don't know exactly how old she is and I don't want to damage her kidneys. And what if the stuff I found wasn't right?

But when I looked in the nest box this morning, there was something that looked like a glass egg. (Although I guess it probably isn't really glass, if Henrietta laid it? It looks like glass and it feels like glass, though. I can't see anything inside, and I can see all the way through it. [Don't worry, I put it in the fridge right away, in the back of the vegetable drawer so my parents wouldn't mess with it.]) So I guess she's a laying hen. She seemed pretty proud of herself, strutting around and squawking her head off when I told her she did a good job. It was a good thing I already told Mom and Dad about her. You could probably hear her all the way at the library.

I still don't know when Great-Uncle Jim bought that food or anything, but it would still be okay for now, right? And I didn't know how many pounds I had, so I couldn't calculate how long it would last me. I couldn't lift the garbage can either, so I had to get my dad to help. Turns out, I have thirty-three pounds of layer crumble in that can (well, a little less because of the can's weight, but I didn't want to empty it to check that), so I should have enough for the whole summer.

I did like the math part. I'm good at math, and you explained how to do it all very clearly. I was pretty sure I got everything right, but I had my mom look it over, just in case, and she said she was very impressed with my work. (My mom doesn't just say things like that.) And my dad liked learning about the diatoms. We made up a song about diatomaceous earth while we were driving in to the post office today, just because we thought it sounded funny. So I guess it was okay in the end.

I'm glad you had a list of what chickens should and shouldn't eat too. I found an old yogurt container to put in the fridge so we can save our scraps for Henrietta

(Great-Uncle Jim really didn't throw anything away, ever, or even recycle it) and I labeled it so Dad wouldn't forget. I'll remind him when we cook and do the dishes too. Mom will like that; she hates to waste things.

I think I'm ready for Lesson 2 now.

Sincerely,
Sophie

PS It was pretty exciting to find that glass egg in the nest box. Like finding a treasure. I love having a chicken.

June 18, 2014

Mr. James Brown
Wherever you are now

Dear Great-Uncle Jim,

Today seemed like it was going to be great. My parents
decided I can keep Henrietta. Mom took a break from
writing and had breakfast with me and Dad, and I made
pancakes that were sort of shaped like chickens, if you
used your imagination. It was sunny, but not too hot, and
I found some old rope in the barn, and Dad even helped
me make a swing out by the henhouse before he had to
go off to his job interview. I'm sorting the pile out there
into different kinds of things so I can find them when I
need them. You could build just about anything out of
all that junk, if you had enough time and imagination
(and could remember which pile the thing you needed
was in). I guess that's why you saved it. Henrietta follows
me around when I carry things from pile to pile, doing
this very quiet cluck, and turning her head to look at
everything. She loves it when there's a bug under a piece
of junk—she pounces on it and gobbles it right up. Then I
sat in the broken chair and read the rest of The Hoboken
Chicken Emergency to Henrietta while she sat in the

dust and fluffed up her feathers. I was worried she'd be scared when the Henrietta in the book has to live all on her own, but she just closed her eyes quietly and listened. I think she really liked it. (I hope this town leaves my Henrietta alone, even though she's unusual too.)

After I took the book back to my room, I was heading to the barn when I heard a horrible noise, almost like a scream, but not human.

I ran as fast as I could, straight to the henhouse. I couldn't see Henrietta anywhere. The door was shut, but I wrenched it open and looked inside. Henrietta was there, glaring at me. I shut the door and latched it again, and just about sat down right there in the dirt and chicken poop, I was so relieved. Henrietta is one smart chicken.

But what had made that sound?

As I looked around, a cloud of crows flew over me, straight for the woods in back of the barn, cawing their heads off. They swooped and flew around a big fir tree, diving at something in the branches.

Well, I've never seen it myself before, but I knew what that meant. Something they thought was bad news was in that tree.

I started toward the tree, but I stopped short as soon as I came around the corner of the barn, and flattened myself to the wall. Ms. Griegson's orange pickup was parked on the old dirt road at the base of the fir tree. Standing next to it, looking up into the branches, was Ms. Griegson.

I don't think she saw me. I took a deep breath and thought for a moment. I was scared, and I was mad, and I wanted her to leave my farm and my chicken alone. But I also wanted to know what she was doing there.

So I stayed where I was and watched the fir tree and Ms. Griegson. There was a big dark shape huddled on a branch, with crows swooping around it. It hopped to a lower branch, and turned to avoid another crow, and I saw it was mottled brown, with reddish tail feathers. I knew that bird from my chicken book. It was a predator, all right: a red-tailed hawk, right here on my farm, just a short ways from my chicken.

Henrietta was safe in her house, I reminded myself, but I didn't feel better. My stomach turned over and over as I looked from the hawk to Ms. Griegson and back. And then Ms. Griegson gave a sharp whistle, and the hawk looked at her too, just as she threw a handful of something on the ground.

The hawk tipped its head to look, just like a chicken. It jumped down off the branch and landed at her feet. A crow swooped down over it, but Ms. Griegson waved it away, and it went back up in the fir with the other crows. The hawk pecked at the ground, and as I watched, it started to change from being all bent over and hooked and sleek to a dark-red chubby chicken, with a huge red comb and a pointy chicken beak and a fluffy chicken butt. It stopped for a minute and crowed, just like in "Old MacDonald," so I guess it was a rooster.

The crows went quiet. Ms. Griegson watched the chicken scratch around for a few minutes. Then she grabbed the dog crate out of the back of her truck and threw another handful inside.

The rooster ran inside the crate, chortling happily. Ms. Griegson shut the door and put the crate back in her truck. She stood and looked around for a minute, and I held my breath in the shadow behind the barn, and was glad I was wearing a brown shirt and muddy jeans. Then she got in the truck and drove off.

I ran right back to check on Henrietta. She was still in the henhouse, and she seemed fine. I left her there.

I know there are unusual chickens now. But I didn't know there were chickens that turned into hawks. My stomach hurts just thinking about it. And what kind of farmer keeps a chicken that turns into a hawk? And drives it around to other people's farms?

I'm scared of that hawk. I'm really scared of Ms. Griegson. But don't worry, that doesn't mean I won't try my hardest to keep Henrietta safe.

Love,
Sophie

PS I followed her truck's tire tracks out to the road and shut the gate tight. I don't know if Dad left it open or if she just opened it herself and drove right in.

PPS It was cracked corn she threw. I checked.

Red-Tailed Hawk to Rhode Island Red

June 18, 2014 (later)

Agnes
Redwood Farm Supply
Gravenstein, CA 95472

Dear Agnes,

Did you sell a rooster that turns into a red-tailed hawk to Ms. Griegson on purpose? If so, I think that was a bad idea. She brought it to my farm today. When it turned into a chicken, it looked like a Rhode Island Red. I don't know what she was doing here, but she didn't get Henrietta.

She didn't get the invisible chicken either. I didn't even see it until after she left. I was nervous, and I went to check behind the barn one more time, and something moved in the grass. It didn't look like a rat, or a squirrel, or even like a chicken. It wasn't that black thing either. It looked like a blurry part of the ground, like a puff of fir needles and leaves and grass blades. I froze, and I waited.

After a long time, slowly, like a spell was wearing off, I saw a shadow of a chicken, and then darker and lighter stripes. A while later, there was a regular-looking fluffy black-and-white chicken pecking at the ground, with a little red comb and yellow legs.

I blinked, and it was still there. So I took a step forward. It vanished.

Well, I couldn't leave it there to wait for Ms. Griegson to come back. So I went and got the old dog crate out of the barn and a handful of sunflower seeds. I couldn't see anything when I got back to the crows' tree, not even a blur, and I felt pretty sad. But I put the crate down anyway, and threw the sunflower seeds inside, and left the door open. After a few minutes, a chicken-sized blur went in, and I slammed the door shut. There was a horrible smell, and I found out invisible chicken poop doesn't stay invisible.

It was heavy and smelly and I was a little worried about what else this special chicken might be able to do, but I carried the crate all the way up to the henhouse anyway.

Henrietta came down from the henhouse and looked hard at the crate. I put it down and I looked hard at it too. I know you said no chicks, but this new chicken looked like a girl chicken, not like a rooster. It's kind of hard to tell when it keeps disappearing, though.

Finally, I gave up worrying about the new chicken and opened the crate door. We both watched while the rest of the sunflower seeds disappeared from inside. I sat very still, and eventually two chickens were pecking around the yard. They seemed like they knew each other. The invisible chicken stayed visible for the rest of the afternoon. Please tell me if it was Great-Uncle Jim's too, so I can tell my parents it turned up and it's my responsibility.

I haven't seen the black one lately.

Sincerely,
Sophie

PS You wouldn't have really sold a hawk-chicken to Ms. Griegson, would you? Did she steal it from you?

PPS Please tell me the hawk-chicken isn't my responsibility too.

Barred Plymouth Rock
(also known as Barred Rock)

Standard height, fluffy black-and-white plumage with distinctive barring, yellow featherless legs and feet. Small red single comb, red earlobes.

Large light-brown eggs, steady layer. Docile and friendly; good for children. Barred coloration helps this breed hide from predators.

Mr. James Brown
Wherever you are now

Dear Great-Uncle Jim,

The disappearing chicken laid an egg this morning!
I could tell it wasn't Henrietta's because it wasn't glass;
it was like a fancy organic brown chicken egg that rich
people buy at the store. I took it out of the nest box really
carefully and put it in the fridge like Agnes said to, even
though I could hardly wait to scramble it and eat it for
breakfast. Maybe she will lay another one, and then in
a few days I can make breakfast for Mom and Dad. They
will just have to agree then that having a chicken is the
best thing ever.

 After I did all my chicken chores and my regular
chores, I checked to see which of my library books were
due. I finally convinced Mom and Dad I could ride my
bike into town on my own, to go to the library. Dad
thought I'd get lost, because he has no sense of direction,
and Mom worried I'd get hit by a car, because she's used
to Los Angeles traffic. They both were afraid I'd get
stuck somewhere in between with no cell-phone service.

But I reminded them that we live here now, and I can't just stay on the farm for the rest of my life, or wait for them to have time to drive me around when I want to go somewhere. I'm twelve, after all, not eight. Sometimes I have things to do. And it's only five miles to town, so even if I got a flat tire or my bike chain fell off, I could walk my bike home. Plus, there's only one road to town, so if they got worried, all they'd have to do is drive in and find me.

They finally agreed, and I promised that if I went anywhere but the library I'd lock my bike up outside so they would see it and could find me if they needed to.

I did ride a little extra carefully into town. The edge of the highway isn't very wide, you know, and people get in a hurry sometimes, and I didn't want to fall down into the grassy ditch next to the road. (Dad says you took him down to catch tadpoles in the ditch in spring, and then they'd turn into frogs, but right now it's too hot and dry to even have water in it.) And there are lots of small hills between our farm and town, so my legs were pretty tired when I got there.

Most of the buildings in town look like they're from old-timey days, maybe when you were young, with those tall fronts that are just for show, like in Wild West movies. There are lots of stores that are just for the tourists; I don't bother with those. I love to look in the window of the bookstore, though. I bet you did too. You sure had a lot of books, all over the living room. But not very many kids' books.

The library is old too, but newer than the rest of the town. I locked my bike up and went inside. Ms. O'Malley helped me find some more chicken books (she thought I'd like one called Prairie Evers, and I think one called The Great Chicken Debacle sounds interesting). I gave her back The Hoboken Chicken Emergency, even though the new chicken hasn't heard it yet. Maybe I'll get it again tomorrow if neither of these is as good.

There was a white girl with brown hair and brown eyes reading in a chair by the window. She looked like she might be about my age, and she was reading a book about llamas. I wonder if she has a llama. She looked up from her book and smiled at me, and I smiled back. But I couldn't think of anything to say to her, and I don't know anything about llamas. So I put the books in my backpack and wheeled my bike up to the feedstore. Maybe I'll see her again sometime. If I do, I'll ask her about llamas, I think. Unless I feel too shy to talk.

I like the feedstore a lot. It's got almost everything—hardware-store stuff and feed and bits of tractors and plants and huge bags of stuff to kill bugs and weeds and cans of paint and even animals. There aren't any chicks right now because it isn't the time of year when they get them, but Jane, who works at the paint counter, says they get hundreds every spring, and sometimes ducklings too. She saw me admiring all the colors of the paint chips and told me I could take some, but I just shook my head. My mom says it isn't right to take things we won't use, even when it's just paint chips. We're still clearing all kinds of things out of the house, so I can't really even see the walls yet. But I already know which one I'd paint my room if we could afford it: it's the most beautiful yellow ever, like baby-chick fluff, and it's called Sunflower Sky. Isn't that a great name?

Anyway. Today I wasn't there just to look around, like when I come in with Dad and he takes forever deciding which kind of wire to get. Today I needed to find out about chicken food and how much it costs. Because even though I already calculated that I have enough food left to feed Henrietta until after school starts, now I have that invisible chicken too. Plus, Agnes says the black streak is one of my chickens too—I just don't know how to go about catching it yet. And I need to have a plan before I tell Mom and Dad about the others.

Chicken food comes in really big bags. I was afraid they would be expensive, but they're mostly under thirty dollars. Of course, that's still expensive for me and for my parents, since we haven't got any money.

I went into the next aisle, with the feeders and waterers and scoops and everything, so I could think. There was a beautiful metal can that said it was a waterer and had a lucky clover on it, and another one that was open on top that said it was a feeder. If I ever have extra money, I'm going to buy them for Henrietta. They would look just right in her henhouse.

As I walked down the aisle, I heard someone asking what to do for her sick chicken. My stomach flopped over funny and I stopped to listen, even though I didn't want to even think about my chickens ever getting sick. I don't know anything about sick chickens, so maybe I could learn what to do.

The person she was talking to sounded exactly like the right person to ask. She was friendly but practical, and she had lots of cheap things to suggest, like baths with Epsom salts and even feeding the chicken some olive oil. She suggested putting the chicken in a quiet dark place by itself for a few days, and said the lady could come back in any time if she needed more help.

They sounded like they were coming closer, and I looked up as they walked by the end of my aisle, still talking.

Great-Uncle Jim, I'm sorry to tell you this, but the really helpful lady was Ms. Griegson.

I hope you don't wish she had your chickens instead of me.

Love,
Sophie

PS I don't want you to take this the wrong way, but I'm glad you can't write back and tell me it would be best if I gave them to her instead of keeping them.

PPS I really am trying to learn as fast as I can.

PPPS Dad didn't get the job. He was pretty upset. I wish he knew enough about farms to work at the feedstore.

PPPPS Maybe I'll get him some more books on farming when I go back to the library tomorrow.

ReDWooD Farm

swdasend with leson2 top drawer

dxdxdxddd

dear sophiie,

you'''re doing great. the new chickenn
is a barred rock. she jjust blends innn,
like a chameleon. she doesn't actually
disappear,herfeatthrs change color. delicious
eggs 7777a7nd lots of them. collect every day
and refrigerate for att least 3 days before
using, just to make sure no chicks develop-
we don't knowwwhere she's been living.,.,.,
the black cochin likes tomatoes.,, good luck
catching her;';';' she's very fast. good eggs
too. sory about the hawk. i gave it to her. but i
didn';"t mean ffor things to turn out like this.
iii will write to some friends 777a7nd see if
they can take the chickens for you/././.. regular
chickens are much easier.

> thank you,..,/.
> agnes

BEGINNER'S CORRESPONDENCE COURSE IN PROPER CARE AND HOUSING FOR POULTRY: CHICKEN EDITION

Lesson 2: Sanitary, Secure Housing

Shelter: At night, chickens' metabolism slows until they are virtually incapable of reacting to predators; they must have a secure place to roost where they will not be attacked. A henhouse:

- Is used for sleeping and laying eggs
- Must be predator-proof (no openings larger than ½ inch)
- Must have a secure latch
- Should be made from suitable materials (untreated wood, metal hardware cloth, etc.)

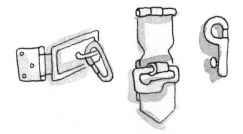

Roosts: Chicken roosts should be sturdy enough to support full-grown hens. Each roost should be:

- Approximately 3 inches in diameter
- Placed over straw, wood shavings, or newspapers (cleaned frequently)
- Sited away from food and water, and not over other roosts
- Long enough to accommodate the entire flock

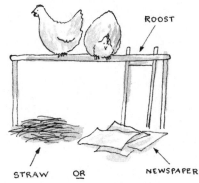

ROOST

STRAW OR NEWSPAPER

Nest boxes: It is not necessary to have a nest box for each hen in the flock, as hens typically lay at different times. Supply 1 nest box per 4 laying hens (consider an extra if allowing a hen to raise chicks from fertile eggs). Boxes should:

- Be dark and quiet
- Be secure on three sides and roofed
- Be lined with straw, wood shavings, etc.
- Provide easy access for daily egg collection

NEST BOXES

Worksheet #2:

Name: _Sophie Brown_____

CALCULATE THE LINEAR FEET OF ROOST SPACE
NEEDED FOR YOUR FLOCK:

I have ~~2~~ 3? chickens.

Each standard-sized adult chicken will use approximately 12 inches (1 linear foot) of roost space.

Therefore, my chickens will need approximately _2_ or 3 _ linear feet of roost space.

(To calculate the amount of roost space needed, multiply 1 linear foot by the number of chickens in your flock.)

CALCULATE THE NUMBER OF NEST BOXES
NEEDED FOR YOUR FLOCK:

I have __2 3?__ laying hens.

Each nest box will serve approximately 4 laying hens.
__2 or 3__ laying hens ÷ 4 = __1__ nest boxes (round up)

Therefore, my flock will need at least __1__ nest boxes.

Please submit your completed worksheet to your instructor in the envelope provided.

Blackbird Farm

June 21, 2014

Agnes
Redwood Farm Supply
Gravenstein, CA 95472

No. Don't you dare send someone to take my chickens. You told me not to give them to anyone. Well, I won't. I don't care if they're harder than regular chickens, and I don't care that I don't already know everything about how to take care of them. You sold them to Great-Uncle Jim, and now I've inherited them. You can't take them back. So don't even think about it.

Sincerely,
Sophie

PS Her name is Chameleon now.

PPS Great-Uncle Jim's henhouse works just fine for his chickens.

PPPS I'm ready for Lesson 3.

June 22, 2014

Mariposa García González
Land of the Dead

Querida Abuelita,

I wish I'd asked you about your chickens while you were
alive. What kind did you have when you were a girl,
before you came to this country? Did you name them,
or just eat them? I know you had to be practical and use
what you had. But if you're still around keeping an eye
on me, would you please keep an eye on my chickens too?
They aren't very good at keeping quiet yet.

Three days ago, Chameleon laid her first egg. I hid
it in the fridge like Agnes said to, so this morning for
breakfast I scrambled it and Mom, Dad, and I each had
two bites. Mom said it was the best egg she'd ever tasted.
And Dad said maybe chickens were pretty useful after
all. (I had to pretend that Henrietta laid the egg, since
they don't know about Chameleon yet, and I don't really
think they're ready to try and understand chickens that
lay glass eggs.) Then we all talked about our favorite egg
recipes, and Dad told me about something Great-Uncle
Jim used to make, called popovers. They're like a really

tall muffin that isn't sweet, that falls over. He said we could make them sometime, if we can find the pan. But your migas is what we all loved best. I wish I could read your recipe, but since I can't, I'm going to look for one at the library. It will be the best surprise ever when I make it for my parents.

After breakfast, when I went to check and make sure Henrietta and Chameleon hadn't dumped their water jars over yet, I saw that black streak chicken again. I've been worried about it. Agnes says it likes tomatoes, but it's not like we can afford to waste tomatoes on a chicken my parents don't know exists and wouldn't necessarily want to catch anyway. I wish Great-Uncle Jim had a garden with tomatoes. Dad was talking about weeding the old vegetable patch the other day, but he didn't get around to it. He doesn't seem to know very much about farms, even though I got him some library books on how to grow things. He spends most of his time walking around the grapevines, shaking his head. By the time we get tomatoes, it will probably be Christmas.

So I used what I had, just like you always taught me. I got sunflower seeds from Great-Uncle Jim's can, and I put them on the ground in a trail leading up to the old dog crate. I thought maybe I could catch and keep it in there until it got used to me. (You'd be proud of me; I did a good job of cleaning the crate after Chameleon pooped in it. It was gross. But I told myself there's no shame in hard work, just like you would have said, and that all the work has to get done by somebody. For a minute, I couldn't remember what your voice sounded like when you said those things, and I was really sad. But now I remember.)

The problem was that Henrietta and Chameleon immediately started eating the seeds themselves. I explained that they were for the black streak chicken, but they just ignored me. So I had to go get more seeds and keep filling in the holes where they ate through the trail. Chameleon vanishes every time Henrietta glares at her. She's getting pretty used to me, though. And the seeds kept disappearing where she'd been, so I knew she hadn't really left.

Anyway, all this ruined my plan to put out the seeds and hide in the bushes and wait. Finally, I just put a whole bunch of seeds out and went to sit in the shade and read my new book. It's pretty good so far. I'm going to read it myself before I read it to the chickens, just in case it might scare them. I was at an exciting part, and you know I don't notice everything around me when I'm reading a good book, so I didn't see the black streak arrive. All I know is that I looked up at the end of the chapter, and three chickens were eating sunflower seeds right in front of me.

The black streak was a chicken, all right, but it was the weirdest-looking chicken I've ever seen. It wasn't much bigger than Henrietta, but it was black, with a little red comb, and its legs and feet were covered in feathers all the way to the ground, like big stompy boots.

All its feathers were weird too—they twisted in every direction, like they'd been blown around in the wind.

I didn't have very long to examine it, though. As soon as it saw me look up, it took off running.

There was no point chasing it, no matter how worried I was about hawk-chickens and people who know a lot about chickens trying to catch it. It's way faster than I am. So I started reading again.

The second time, I saw it run out of the woods, screech to a halt, and start eating, just like that roadrunner in the cartoons. I tried to pretend it wasn't there. It had a drink of water. Then it had some more sunflower seeds. Then it got too close to Henrietta, and she glared at it. It floated a few inches off the ground, its feathery boots moving fast, just out of reach of the sunflower seeds. I wished I could tell Henrietta to put it in the crate, but she's not exactly a trained superchicken. Henrietta went back to eating her seeds, and as she stopped glaring at it, the black streak chicken floated gently down. It looked at her for a minute, then moved off a bit and started eating seeds again.

I hope it's still there when I go check on them after dinner. I can't exactly keep it from running off, but maybe it will remember this is its home. At least I got to see what it looks like.

Te quiero,
Soficita

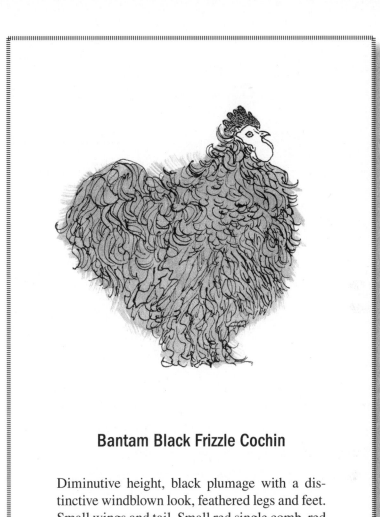

Bantam Black Frizzle Cochin

Diminutive height, black plumage with a distinctive windblown look, feathered legs and feet. Small wings and tail. Small red single comb, red earlobes.

Small light-brown eggs, infrequent layer. Friendly and inquisitive when hand-raised.

Mr. James Brown
Wherever you are now

Dear Great-Uncle Jim,

I guess it's a good thing I like unusual chickens, because they keep turning up. It's really too bad you're dead, because I have an awful lot of questions for you.

You already know Henrietta came to live with me, and a chameleon chicken turned up too, and I think the black streak chicken has decided to stay. (I might as well name her Roadrunner, since I already think of her that way.) Except, you know, I haven't told my parents about the new ones yet.

Well, when I came inside this afternoon, Dad was studying your antique phone (you know, the weird black one on the wall) like he was about to take it apart. Maybe he got that from you. Things don't always go back together in quite the same way when Dad's worked on them for a while, so normally I'd be a little nervous, but I don't have any friends here to call, so I guess he can go for it if he wants to.

"Sophie, Gregory at the post office called for you." He handed me a slip of paper.

My stomach felt funny. I like Gregory, but why would he call me when he'll be delivering the mail tomorrow anyway? I meet him every day at the mailbox, since I can see him driving up from the barn window. Usually good news can wait, and bad news can't. I looked at the number for a long time. Then I looked at the really old phone on the wall. "Dad, how do you dial this thing?"

Dad told me to put the cone-on-a-string part up to my ear and just talk really loudly at the cone part stuck onto the phone on the wall. He got me a stool so my mouth would be at the right height, and I stuck my fingers in the holes and moved the dial around. Gregory picked up right away.

"Hello, is this Gregory?" I asked. "This is Sophie Brown."

"Hello, Sophie," Gregory said. "I think I found another one of Jim Brown's chickens while I was doing my deliveries, but it needs to be picked up today. Can you go get it, or do you want me to ask and see if someone else can take it?"

I bit my lip. It was nice of Gregory to try and help us out—I've told him before that my parents aren't that into farm animals—but if this really was one of your special chickens, Agnes would expect me to make sure it was safely with the rest. Probably whoever Gregory could find to take it wouldn't have special chickens, and I bet regular chickens weren't going to like living with this one, if it was anything like Henrietta. Unless it was Ms. Griegson he was thinking of. "Can you hang on for just a minute while I ask my dad?"

I wasn't quite sure what part of the phone to cover, but I did my best. I thought really fast. I didn't want to lie, but I didn't want Dad to say no either. "Dad, more of Great-Uncle Jim's chickens turned up. Gregory says we need to pick them up today. If we can't afford to take responsibility for them, he'll try to find someone else who can." (I figured I might as well get the other two cleared up at the same time.)

Dad looked pretty mad. I know he hates it when people think we might need special help. (I felt bad about making him mad on purpose, but really, these chickens need to be safe.) He stomped over to the doorway to Mom's study and yanked the door open. Mom's writing music blasted out into the hall.

My stomach settled down a little bit and I started to think again. Mom hates charity even more than Dad does, so I thought maybe things would be okay. (People always think Mom and I are poor. They even did when we had some money, just because we're brown. Mom's used to it, but it still makes her mad, even more so now that we really are poor. I don't think Dad will ever get used to it.)

I picked up the pencil from the hall table and uncovered the phone. "Thanks for waiting, Gregory. Where should we pick the chicken up?"

There was a long pause, and then Gregory said, "Sophie, do you know anything about how to keep these kinds of chickens?"

He hadn't told me what breed of chicken it was. But I knew exactly what he meant. So Gregory knew about Great-Uncle Jim's unusual chickens. But Agnes said I couldn't tell anyone, and that included Gregory. I wasn't going to mess things up now.

I took a deep breath. "Yes," I said. Maybe I didn't know all about chicken diseases and Epsom salts and all of that, but Agnes was teaching me about special chickens, and as far as I could tell, I knew as much about them as anyone else around. Except maybe Ms. Griegson. But you know what Agnes thinks about that. It's my responsibility to protect your chickens.

"Yes, I do," I said.

There was another long pause, so long I thought maybe the phone had stopped working. I wasn't sure what I'd do if I didn't pass Gregory's test. Why had he called me if he didn't think I could take care of this new chicken?

And then Gregory sighed. "Just be careful, okay?"

I wrote down directions while Mom and Dad argued some more. By the time they came out to tell me I'd have to take care of the new chickens too, I already had all the information. So I dutifully told Gregory my parents had agreed, and he hung up so he could call and let the people who'd found the chicken know I'd be coming for her.

Dad looked at his watch and sighed. "I'm already late to meet Bob about that replacement tractor key. Sophie, it's just going to have to wait until I'm back."

"No problem, Dad," I said, and gave him a hug as Mom walked back into her study and turned the music back up.

I gave it about ten minutes, long enough for Mom to be wrapped up in her work again. Then I knocked on her door and asked if I could walk over and pick the chickens up myself, since it was only a mile away.

"Sure, whatever, just give me another fifteen minutes," Mom said, not looking up.

So I decided I better go get that chicken before Dad comes back and Mom remembers what she agreed to. (Don't worry, I'll leave a note reminding her where I went.) Only, I'm nervous. What if Ms. Griegson turns up there too? What if these people don't think I look responsible enough? I guess this is just another part of keeping chickens.

Love,
Sophie

Mariposa García González

Land of the Dead

Querida Abuelita,

I guess I never really was afraid of a chicken before.
I mean, I didn't want to get pecked, and Henrietta made
me a little nervous a few times when she looked at me too
long, but I'm bigger than she is, and I think I'd be hard
for her to lift. But this newest chicken . . . Well, I think
it's better if you don't tell Mom or Dad about her
superpowers until I find out more.

I sort of thought it was just going to be another
chicken with regular superpowers when Gregory called.
I was happy that this chicken would be back with the
rest of her flock; I didn't want her to be lonely. I thought
I'd just walk over there, with the dog crate in the old red
wagon, and bring her back, and everything would be as
normal as it ever is around here.

When I got to the farm, a white dog came rushing
out to the gate and barked and barked, but I hollered I
was here for the chicken, and didn't open the gate, and
finally a skinny blond lady came out. She looked at me
for a long time, and I got more and more nervous. You

know I'm pretty shy around people I don't know. It's like all my words get clogged up in my throat, even when it's important and I know I have to say something. "Gregory said you were coming," she said, finally. She grabbed the dog's collar, opened the gate, and told me to go around the back of the barn. Then she dragged the dog inside.

I was feeling a little shaky, the way you do when you're not sure if someone's mad at you, or why they'd be mad when you haven't even met them before. But things weren't going to get any better standing around in her yard. So I dragged that rattling old wagon around the back of the barn.

There was a boy sitting there, about my age. He was staring at a chicken coop across the yard, leaning his chin against his knees, and he looked scared and sad. Then he saw me and scowled, and I stopped feeling sorry for him, even if his mom didn't seem very nice.

I've never been the new kid before. But I figured it wasn't going to get any easier without practice. "I'm Sophie Brown," I said. "I'm here to pick up Great-Uncle Jim's chicken. Thanks for taking care of her."

He didn't move, just kept scowling.

"Gregory called to say I should come get her?" I said. I didn't scowl back, even though I wanted to.

"You know she's weird?" he said very quietly.

"I know she's unusual," I snapped. Then I was horrified at what I'd said. But he didn't ask any questions, just nodded, got up, and led me around the back of the coop.

There were two small pens there, and both of them had big bloody pieces of burlap inside. The burlap didn't cover all the blood and mess either. Abuelita, I know a farm is a cycle of life and death, and I know where meat comes from. I know that bad things happen to animals sometimes. But it was really horrible, with bits of bloody meat and bone and feathers all over. I looked at it, and then I grabbed the kid's arm and started yelling at him. "Why did you kill her? What did she ever do to you?"

His face got all crumpled and he looked like he was going to cry. "A raccoon got Rocky this morning."

It took a few seconds for the words to start making sense. I dropped his arm. "Who named her Rocky?"

"Rocky's a rooster, not a hen. I raised him from a chick." He looked down at the blood in one of the pens. "The raccoon's over there." He pointed inside.

I looked closer. There was a stone raccoon inside the chicken pen with a messy chicken leg in its paws. I stared at it. Who would want to carve such a horrible thing?

"My mom heard the noise and came running. Rocky was already dead. The raccoon was—like that—and Buffy's chicks were all staring up at it, so Mom grabbed the shovel and . . . I'm sorry." He looked away.

I felt the goose bumps run all over my skin. "What about the hen?"

"Buff Orpington, good layer, a little shy, one extra point on the comb but still show-worthy. I was going to show her this year—she's the only hen I have. We called her Buffy," he said automatically. Then his face got unhappy. "She wasn't in with her chicks. . . . Mom found her dust-bathing under the blueberries. She never did anything like . . . whatever they did. But Mom shut her in a crate and told Gregory she has to go."

Well, I could understand why, if her chicks did that. But she was my responsibility now. I squared my shoulders. "Okay. Can I borrow the crate? You can have mine until I can bring it back."

The kid looked at me then, like he was kind of impressed. "Sure," he said. He led me over to a dog crate that was covered with more burlap. At least this wasn't bloody. I grabbed my crate out of the wagon and put it down, and the kid put the burlap-covered crate in the wagon. The chicken inside squawked, so I guess she was all right.

"Does she have water and food?" I asked.

The boy shrugged. "Mom wouldn't let me open it," he said.

"Well, she has to have water, at least," I said stubbornly. I know chickens can die fast without water. "Give it to me, and I'll do it."

So he gave me an old yogurt container full of water, and I opened the crate door without lifting the burlap, stuck the water inside, and shut the door again as fast as I could.

The boy watched all this in silence. Then he looked at me and said, "I'm Chris. See you around sometime." He went off inside before I thought of anything else to say.

I know you would never approve of messing with someone else's property. But, Abuelita, that raccoon statue was so horrible. And it was pretty clear that boy wanted nothing to do with it. And, also, maybe this is selfish of me, but I didn't want people to come after this new chicken with pitchforks, like they did with Frankenstein. I'm pretty sure it wasn't her fault, whatever happened.

I pushed the statue in their pond. I'm sure they could get it out again if they really wanted to, but it was heavy and horrible and I can't think why they'd want to. Don't worry, I wore my gloves. And I don't think I messed up the ground too bad pushing it. (It was really heavy.)

That chicken sure was noisy. I don't think she liked the wagon. But we made it home. I put her crate in the barn and stuck some food inside, but I latched her door closed again. I don't know what to do. I don't want her to turn the other chickens to stone, or me, or my parents. But I can't leave her in there forever. I hope that Agnes writes back soon.

Te quiero,
Soficita

PS I wish I'd told that boy I was sorry about his rooster, and his chicks. I feel bad about that.

PPS How did Gregory know the chicken was Great-Uncle Jim's? Why am I not supposed to tell anyone if everyone here already knows about them? Does Gregory know that Chris knows too?

Blackbird Farm

June 23, 2014

Agnes

Redwood Farm Supply

Gravenstein, CA 95472

Dear Agnes,

Sorry to bother you, but I really need to know about Great-Uncle Jim's Buff Orpington hen. There's a nasty stone raccoon statue at Chris Smith's farm now, and I don't have a good feeling about it. Should I ask Gregory to give this one to someone else after all?

Sincerely,
Sophie

PS Ms. Smith killed her chicks. I'm sorry.

PPS I pushed the statue in the pond.

PPPS Please don't say I have to kill the hen.

PPPPS Why do you sell dangerous chickens like that? Someone could get hurt.

ReDwooD Farm

dddear sophie

buff orpington = cockatrice hatcher, not cockatrice herself. shuldnot turn anyonne to st0one,,. might glare alot,.do not evr ever keep iwth aany rooster. especiially not sue'''s,,,. collct eggs evry singleday aand refrigeratte fr next 30 dayys,,. safe to eat affter 3 days innn fridge,. might contain sand;; wattch youur teeth,.

very importantlllldo not give that chickn toanyone else,,.,.obviously,,,. i don't sellll her kind. they'''re very rare,.,.,. chicks aare dangeererous. i trustedd jim.

thnk you for savving her,,.

agnesss

otherss;
3 speckled sussex hens
think that''s aall jim had lefft

Buff Orpington

Standard height; large, rounded body; golden brown plumage; clean legs and feet. Small red single comb, red earlobes.

Large light-brown eggs, frequent layer. Very docile. Will often go broody; excellent for raising chicks from fertile eggs.

June 25, 2014

Mariposa García González
Land of the Dead

Querida Abuelita,

I saw a flyer at the library yesterday, for the 4-H
poultry program. It had a picture of funny-looking
chickens on it, with feathery pom-poms on their heads.
I didn't know what 4-H was, but I looked it up and
it's for kids to learn about farm things. And I want
to learn about poultry, or at least chickens. It said it
meets on the last Wednesday of the month, which is
today, and it's for ages ten to fourteen, which is me,
and maybe also this boy named Chris that I met, the
one whose rooster got killed. Maybe even that girl with
the llama book, that I haven't really met yet. And it's
free. And, Abuelita, none of my old friends write to me.
So I asked if I could go.

When Dad dropped me off at the library, I was a
little nervous. I don't really like meeting new people.
And when I have to talk to a group, it's like my throat is
strangling on the inside and I can't breathe. But I don't
like not knowing anyone either. So I thought about my

chickens, and I went inside and asked Ms. O'Malley where the meeting room was.

She gave me kind of a funny look when she told me. The kind of look that made my stomach hurt. But I told myself that if you could be brave when you first came to LA, I could be brave here.

When I got to the meeting room, there were already a bunch of kids inside, and they all looked like they knew each other, and almost none of them were brown. But I figured that's how it would be. I saw the girl with the llama book, though, and she smiled at me again. So I took a deep breath, and I got ready to answer all kinds of questions as soon as I went in—who I was, when I came here, that I speak English just fine, that Great-Uncle Jim was really my great-uncle, even though I don't look like him, that yes, I have some chickens (but not too much about the chickens)—and then I heard a voice. I don't think I could have moved even if I wanted to. I just looked inside, and there, at the head of the room, writing stuff on the board, was Ms. Griegson. She turned her head, and I ducked back out the doorway. I left so fast I was almost running, all the way back down the hall to the main part of the library. I know she probably wouldn't have chased me. But I sure didn't want her to see me there.

I went and read about chickens in the green chair in the corner of the library. Ms. O'Malley saw me, though. I know because she brought over the local newspaper and asked if I'd seen the article about Redwood Farm Supply. So I read it. Only it wasn't about Redwood Farm Supply. It was about Ms. Griegson saying she'd always wanted to be the owner of Redwood Farm Supply, and now she's working to reopen it, making Gravenstein a destination spot for poultry lovers everywhere.

What is she talking about, Abuelita? Agnes owns Redwood Farm Supply. She wouldn't sell it to Ms. Griegson, even if she did sell that hawk-chicken to her. At least, I hope she wouldn't.

I'm worried. I know Ms. Griegson knows a lot more about chickens than I do. I know she wants my chickens too.

I read about chickens until it was time for Dad to come pick me up. Then I went and met him outside before the kids or Ms. Griegson could come out of the meeting room. When he asked me how it was, I said it was fine. Dad has enough to worry about. But I'm not going back to 4-H.

> Te extraño mucho,
> Soficita

GRAVENSTEIN INDEPENDENT JOURNAL

June 24, 2014

NEW LIFE FOR REDWOOD FARM SUPPLY?

by Joy Ocampo

"Unusual chickens have been my life's work ever since I first worked for Redwood Farm Supply," said Sue Griegson, who has begun the process to try to buy Redwood Farm Supply and bring the company back to life, putting Gravenstein once again on the poultry map.

Continued on p. 10

Blackbird Farm

Mr. James Brown
Wherever you are now

Dear Great-Uncle Jim,

I think your chickens are doing okay now. I bet you miss
them a lot. I give them new food and water every single
morning, even though I need to use a lot of your jars to
make sure all the chickens have plenty. There's a lot of
poop too, but it's no big deal; I just clean it up and put some
new straw in. I wish I had another block of straw for when
the one in the barn runs out, but I'll think of something.

   Every morning, I check the nest boxes for
eggs. Usually there aren't any, and that's kind of
disappointing. But this morning there were two eggs
in one nest box: one glass one and one light-brown one.
I was so excited. I really wished I could show someone.
But at least I can tell you about it. Here is a picture of the
eggs in the nest box, just for you.

I hid them in the fridge in one of your old plastic containers. It was for margarine, and you can't see inside it unless you take the lid off. I don't think anyone will look in there.

And I read to them every afternoon. I know they probably don't understand, but my cousin Lupe wants to be a teacher and she says you're supposed to read to babies, and they don't understand either, so I figure it can't hurt. I haven't seen that Ms. Griegson lately. Maybe she gave up bothering us.

I was pretty scared of Buffy until I got Agnes's letter. Now I know only her chicks could turn things to stone, but still . . . I don't have a chicken that can turn stone things back to life, and Agnes didn't say it wears off. I was pretty surprised you had her at all. But then I thought maybe it's like zoos. I mean, you need someone responsible to make sure we still have tigers. You wouldn't want them to go extinct.

I wish Agnes would tell me more about Buffy. Agnes seems kind of disorganized to be running a chicken business. She has a lot of problems with her typewriter too. You'd think she'd just write things out. But maybe no one can read her handwriting, like with my grandmother.

When I got Buffy, I got her from a boy who lives near here called Chris who says he knew you. It makes me feel kind of funny, only not really funny, but sad, and maybe a little mad, to think about how he knew you better than I did. Anyway, he came over yesterday. He brought my crate back, and I gave him his. Good thing I'd cleaned it out already. My dad came to find me while I was out making sure Buffy was getting along okay with the other chickens, and he'd brought Chris back with him. I know, I worry about my dad too, sometimes; he's awfully trusting. You'd think he'd never heard of chicken thieves. Anyway, Chris's eyes went big and round when he saw Henrietta and the others. But they all had plenty of food and water, so I hoped they would just keep scratching in the dust like regular chickens.

I figured he probably wanted to make sure his chicken was okay (even though really she was your chicken, and therefore really my chicken). I remember what it felt like when I thought I'd lose Henrietta, and I'd only just met her. So I said hi and tried not to be suspicious or mad, and after Dad went off toward the vineyards, we sat and talked about chickens for a while. Chris told me about poultry shows, where you bring your chickens for everyone to see, and talk about them in front of everybody, and all the kinds of chickens that folks on the farms around here have. There's a kind called a Silkie, a little bantam chicken that only has fluff, no feathers, and Chris says they probably can't really even see very well, because they're so covered in fluff they look like Muppets, not like chickens. Like big lumpy chicks, I guess. And you have to keep them inside all winter, or they get too wet and cold, even in California, on account of them not having proper feathers. (I told Chris I didn't have to worry about that sort of thing, having a whole empty barn and all, and he looked pretty jealous to hear about it. He has a barn too, but it's full of sheep in the winter, which aren't nearly as interesting as chickens.) But I guess you probably know all about Silkies already, raising unusual chickens and all. Chris said you even used to take some of your chickens to the poultry shows. I wanted to ask if he'd ever seen any of them do anything unusual, or why nobody noticed, but I'm not sure how well he knows Ms. Griegson. I decided I'd better get to know him first. (I kind of wanted to take my chickens to a show, until I found out you have to talk in front of everybody, and sometimes it costs money to show them. Now I just want to go see other people's chickens.)

Anyway, it turns out Chris likes to draw. He drew a picture of my henhouse on the stumps, only it wasn't really realistic, because he drew it walking through the woods, like the stumps were feet, and you know that's impossible. It made me laugh, though. So he drew another, with Henrietta leaning out the front door like a pilot and Buffy clinging to the roof. We've decided to make a comic book, and I'm going to do the writing. Here's a copy of the first part for you. See what I mean? He's pretty good.

I didn't tell him anything more about the chickens, though. Don't worry. I don't think he'd tell. But I know I have to keep them safe.

Love,
Sophie

PS Chris showed me how to wind up the rope swing that my dad made and get on and let it spin around and around until you're so dizzy you feel like you might throw up and have to lie down until everything stops moving. It was great.

PPS Since you left us so much rope, I'm going to see if my dad will make another swing in the other tree, for when I have friends over.

PPPS Chris says you can grow sunflowers from sunflower seeds, and then you can save the seeds from the sunflowers for your chickens! So you plant one seed, and harvest a whole bunch! I'm going to plant some right away. I bet that's how you got so many.

PPPPS When I told Gregory I got your chicken from Chris, he just nodded and said "Good," and asked if I had any letters to mail today.

June 26, 2014

Agnes
Redwood Farm Supply
Gravenstein, CA 95472

Dear Agnes,

When I went to the feedstore today, after I took my
library books back, Jane who works there asked if by any
chance I'd found any small glass eggs around Great-Uncle
Jim's farm. She says he used to sell them to the feedstore,
to fool people's chickens into laying. I guess he told her
once he had lots left over from a project a long time ago.
Well, I don't know about you, but that sounds exactly like
Henrietta's eggs to me. Would it be okay if I sold them
to the feedstore, as long as I didn't say where they were
from? Great-Uncle Jim had so much junk around that no
one would know but me, really. No one could make them
hatch if I refrigerated them for three days first, could
they? I've collected a few, and I found some more in one
of Great-Uncle Jim's blue jars in the back of the cupboard
under the sink. I didn't know for sure if he'd put them
in the fridge, so I put them in just to be sure. Jane said
they'd pay me a dollar each. And with four chickens now,

that food is disappearing a lot faster than it used to.

Jane gave me a flyer for the town poultry show too—it's less than a week away! She said it was too late to enter chickens into the show, but I should come anyway so I'd know what to expect at the next one. Jane's nice. I didn't tell her it wouldn't be a good idea to bring my chickens to a show.

She said something funny, though, so I thought I'd ask you about it. When I asked her if Redwood Farm Supply would be there, she told me they'd gone out of business years ago. Well, I knew that wasn't true, but I wondered if maybe you only secretly sell chickens now, because of Ms. Griegson and the typewriter and all. So I kept my mouth shut. I figured you'd appreciate that.

I think I might go to the show even if I can't bring any chickens. I've never been to a poultry show before. I wonder if Chris will be there. I guess he probably already knows everyone, and all their chickens too.

> Still your friend,
> Sophie

PS Did you see that article about Ms. Griegson wanting Redwood Farm Supply? What was that all about? You wouldn't sell it to her, would you?

PPS Please do let me know right away if I can sell Henrietta's eggs.

GRAVENSTEIN POULTRY ASSOCIATION

23RD ANNUAL
POULTRY SHOW

Open / Youth / 4-H

APA / ABA Sanctioned

APA Licensed Judges:
Sue Griegson & Grace O'Malley

Also featuring children's poultry presentations
(unjudged, free, very educational)

July 1st, 2014   **6–8 p.m.**

(setup begins at 4 p.m.)

Held in the Gravenstein Veterans Memorial Building
and Luther Burbank Park (adjoining)

Trailer hookups available

For more information, call (707) 823-7691,
or stop by the Gravenstein Public Library to pick up an entry form.
Show entry forms and fees must be received no later than June 13, 2014.

***Please note that space is limited for ostriches, emus, and rheas.
Turn your forms in as soon as possible to reserve your space!***

Blackbird Farm

June 28, 2014

Agnes
Redwood Farm Supply
Gravenstein, CA 95472

Dear Agnes,

I forgot to tell you before, but I wanted you to know I've
been putting every single egg in the fridge every day,
especially now that I know how important it is. For a
while, I didn't know exactly whose was whose, since the
chickens all lay in the same nest box and they're kind of
sneaky about it, but I think I know now: the little glass
eggs are Henrietta's, the regular-size light-brown eggs
that are kind of pointy are Chameleon's, the little light-
brown eggs that aren't there very often are Roadrunner's
(I do hope she's not laying them somewhere else while
she runs around, but I've looked and looked and haven't
found any), and I don't think Buffy has laid any yet.
I have a list and a whole system for making sure they
stay in the fridge long enough before I cook them, kind of
like Mom's system for her article deadlines.

    I think it would be okay to sell Henrietta's eggs, since
they've been in the fridge, and since Great-Uncle Jim did

used to sell them. But I would feel better if you let me know for sure. Will you please write back?

Sincerely,

Sophie

PS I'm still waiting for Lesson 3 too.

PPS What do the Speckled Sussex do?

PPPS And where could they be? Should I go look for them?

June 29, 2014

Mariposa García González
Heaven's Dance Party

Querida Abuelita,

I made migas for Mom and Dad last night for dinner.
Mom was so surprised. Dad said it was the best migas
ever—even better than yours. I explained that that's
because the eggs were so fresh.

I asked Mom why you made migas, since my library
book said it was really from Texas, and you never lived
in Texas. And Mom told me the story of how you learned
to make it from Señora Armandariz, who worked at the
bank, and how Mom and Tío Fernando used to beg you to
make it when they were my age. "But it never occurred
to me to learn how!" she said.

She gave me a big hug and said she was so proud
of me. Then she even called Tío Fernando's and told
everyone about my migas, and Tía Catalina asked me
to email her the recipe for their next Sunday meal,
and Lupe and Javier wanted to know if I really have
chickens. It was kind of embarrassing. But also kind
of nice.

After dinner, I asked if we could have a family dance party and dance off our migas, even though we aren't at Tío Fernando's and it's just us. So we moved all the furniture around the living room and Dad sang along to "Three Little Birds" while Mom and I danced. (Dad makes a really funny Bob Marley. Don't tell him I said so.) Then Mom picked "Sabotage" and we did our hip-hop moves, and Mom covered my ears when they sang the bad word, just like Tía Catalina always did, except she made it like a cool dance move.

I picked "Kiss," because it's fun to dance to and because Dad is an even funnier Prince. (Not because I want to kiss anyone. Ew.) And then Dad remembered this really funny song called "The Funky Chicken" and taught me and Mom how to do the dance. Sometimes Dad is really old-school. And last of all we put on "Quizás, Quizás, Quizás" because it was your favorite, and we all sang along with Celia Cruz and did the salsa, and even though my dad makes the funniest Celia of all, I still cried. But it was the good kind of crying.

This morning, I told the chickens that my parents said their eggs were delicious, and that all the rest of my family wanted to have some too, and to know all about them. They seemed pretty pleased to hear it. (I didn't tell Henrietta that of course I couldn't use hers, but don't worry, I know better than to try to cook glass eggs.)

Maybe I'll make migas for Chris sometime, if he

comes over again. I saw him at the library yesterday, and he said fresh eggs are his favorite food, but he's never had migas. (He says he makes omelets with tons and tons of cheese.) I wish you could come have some of my migas too.

Te extraño mucho,
Soficita

MIGAS

like Señora Armandariz and my abuelita used to make

Migas means "crumbs."
So you're supposed to use leftovers when you make it.
It's that kind of recipe.

Ingredients:

- Eggs (about twice as many eggs as you have people
  who want to eat migas, give or take a few)
- Salsa (maybe a quarter cup, or whatever you have left
  over; not too spicy, unless you like things spicy)
- Oil (whatever kind you have around that's for cooking)
- Corn tortillas (about as many as you have people who
  want to eat migas), cut up into little pieces. (It's okay
  if they're a little stale. You could even cut up your
  leftover tortillas after you have tacos or quesadillas
  and put them in the freezer to save for migas, if you
  were organized. My abuelita used to do this.)

- Other good stuff you might have around, like grated cheese or chopped tomatoes or sliced olives or cut-up avocado

Instructions:

1. Crack the eggs into a bowl.

2. Pour whatever leftover salsa you have into the eggs and mix it all up with a fork. If it isn't as salsa-y as you want this time, don't eat so many chips and salsa next time, and save more for migas.

3. Put oil in your big frying pan. (Not so much that it sloshes around or anything, but enough to cover the bottom of the pan, because otherwise things will stick, and that's really a big pain to clean out.) Put the pan on the stove and turn on the stove to medium or so.

4. Put the cut-up tortillas in the pan. Stir them around with a wooden spoon until they get soft. It's okay if they get kind of crispy, but don't let them burn.

5. Once your tortillas are fried but not burnt, turn the stove down to low. Wait for a couple of minutes so the pan cools off some. Then you can pour in your mixed-up eggs and salsa, and very carefully stir them around until the eggs are cooked.

6. Turn the stove off. If you have any cheese or olives or cut-up avocado or anything, you can add it on top now, but you don't really need anything else. Get yourself a fork and try a little bite. If you feel like it needs a little something, add some salt and/or pepper.

7. When it tastes good to you, get as many plates as you need and serve up some migas. (If you had extra flour tortillas, you could roll your migas up like breakfast burritos. We did that once at my friend Pilar's house. It was so good!)

8. When you put the migas on the table, you can say "¡Buen provecho!" just like my abuelita always said.

Agnes
Redwood Farm Supply
Gravenstein, CA 95472

Dear Agnes,

Why haven't you written back to me yet? Are you mad at me? Did I do something wrong?

I was worried, so I asked Gregory the mailman if he'd given you my letters. Maybe I shouldn't have asked, because he looked kind of funny, but he told me yes, he was certain he'd delivered all my letters, just like he always does, and no, there'd been no letters from you to deliver to me. He told me he always makes certain to deliver your letters to me as soon as he can, because I'm one of his best customers, writing so often and all. (I know really he delivers everyone's letters equally, because you have to be fair when you work for the post office, and Gregory is a very fair person who takes his job seriously. But I appreciated him saying so.) Maybe you went out of town and you forgot to tell me.

I hope you're okay. I hope Ms. Griegson's rooster didn't get you, or your own chickens. Maybe you have the flu. Even my mom can't write when she has the flu. Even when she's on deadline. And my mom prides herself on being timely and responsible.

Still your friend,
Sophie

PS I didn't mean to say you weren't responsible.

PPS Maybe you've been really busy getting ready for the poultry show and I'll finally meet you there tomorrow?

PPPS I did sell Henrietta's eggs to the feedstore. I needed to. I hope you understand.

June 30, 2014 (later)

Agnes

Redwood Farm Supply

Gravenstein, CA 95472

Dear Agnes,

We have a problem. We have to save some of my chickens.

That boy Chris rode by our house today, just before dinner. I was out in the front yard, pulling up dandelions for the chickens to peck at, so I waved.

He stopped, and we chatted for a while. He asked if I was going to the poultry show tomorrow, and I said I thought so, and he said that was good, because he was going to have a surprise to show there. (I hope it isn't an unusual surprise.)

Then he looked kind of funny. He leaned over the fence and whispered, "I think Ms. Griegson stole three of Mr. Brown's chickens."

I probably looked kind of funny then myself. I was shocked, and scared, and glad he told me, and also nervous about what to do about it.

"Not your chickens," he said. "The other ones Mr. Brown had. I go to all the shows, and I pay attention, and I know that Ms. Griegson only ever has Rhode Island

Reds, and that Mr. Brown had three Speckled Sussex that he brought to the show, even though one of them had a pecked wattle and one of them had a mottled beak and the third had black eyes, and they never took any prizes. They must be four years old now, but I'd know them anywhere."

"Where is she keeping them?" I asked. I was thinking hard. If they were Great-Uncle Jim's chickens, and you aren't supposed to keep special chickens in with the other kind, and he'd had them for years, well, then these were special chickens too.

Chris looked kind of shifty-eyed then. "You're not from around here, so I don't know if you know . . . but you don't go on other people's farms without permission. Not without a really good reason, like a fire, or an escaped sheep, something like that. But it was my mom's birthday yesterday, and she was having a bad week. She's not real patient sometimes, but she tries. So . . . ," he trailed off.

I just waited. I learned that from my mom, that sometimes you just have to give people enough space to have their say, without jumping right in with whatever you think, even if you have a whole lot of thinking on that very subject. I'm not sure my dad will ever learn that; it's not his style. But it works for me and my mom.

He sighed. "There's a big patch of flowers that no one seems to know about on the back corner of Ms. Griegson's farm, up by the pond. She doesn't have sheep, so they don't get eaten. I went to pick some for my mom, and I knew Ms. Griegson was up at her job in town, so I didn't ask permission. When I got there, I saw that she's got a new henhouse and pen by the pond, apart from the Rhode Island Reds. So I looked. Your chickens are up there." He hesitated.

I waited some more.

"It's really big for just three chickens," he said unhappily.

I shivered. I thought hard for a while. It would be better to handle this myself, in case I got in trouble. But it would take too long for me to sort it out on my own. So I asked him, "Will you show me where they are?"

He hesitated for so long I thought he was going to say no. But he nodded. "Meet me tomorrow afternoon at three, right here," he said. "And cross your fingers she'll be off setting up cages for the poultry show."

I looked at the sky, feeling all sorts of wriggling anxious thoughts, but even I knew it was getting too dark to go tonight. So I nodded. I hope he doesn't chicken out on me.

When you get this, I need to know right away: what is special about Great-Uncle Jim's three Speckled Sussex? Hopefully, they aren't too dangerous if he took them to the fair every year? Do you think you could call me, just this once? Great-Uncle Jim's phone number is (707) 823-2618.

Sophie

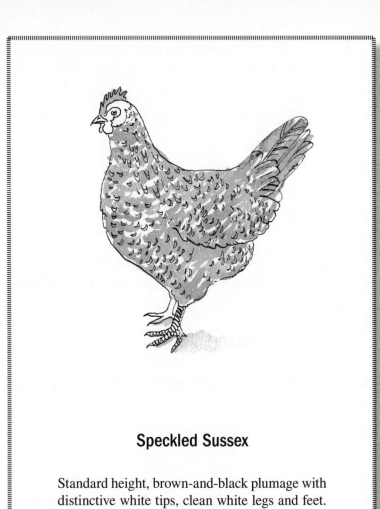

Speckled Sussex

Standard height, brown-and-black plumage with distinctive white tips, clean white legs and feet. Small red single comb, red earlobes.

Large light-brown eggs, frequent layer. Chatty and sociable; will often follow farmers around.

Blackbird Farm

July 1, 2014

Agnes

Redwood Farm Supply

Gravenstein, CA 95472

Dear Agnes,

This afternoon, after I did all my chicken chores, I told my parents I was going for a bike ride with Chris, and yes, of course I'd wear my helmet, and my whistle, and bring my cell phone, and that I might go to the poultry show with him, but I'd call if I wouldn't be back by dinner.

Then I went to get ready. I knew I had a problem. I wasn't going to just leave my chickens on Ms. Griegson's farm, even if they weren't chickens I'd met yet. And I had no real right to take them.

First, I stuffed my pockets full of sunflower seeds. Then I pulled the rattling old wagon and the smelly dog crate around and parked them next to my bike. (I meant to wash the crate right after Henrietta pooped in it the other day, but I was trying to make sure Buffy settled in okay with Henrietta and the others—oh, you know.)

I was looking to see how I could hitch the wagon to

my bike without the handle getting stuck in the spokes or dragging on the ground, when Chris rode up.

Chris took one look at it and shook his head. "No way," he said. "You can take that thing if you want to, but I'm not going with you."

"But how am I going to get the chickens back?" I asked reasonably. "I can't exactly carry them all on my bike."

He shook his head again. "That's not the deal," he said. "I'll show you where Ms. Griegson's farm is, because that's neighborly. I'll show you where she's got your chickens, because that's the right thing to do. But there's no way I'm getting caught helping you steal chickens. My mom would never let me leave the house again if she heard about it, and you can be sure she'd hear all about it."

I must have frowned pretty hard, because he looked at my face and he swallowed a few times, but he wasn't budging. Now, I don't really blame him—I'd met his mom, and I wouldn't want her mad at me either—but I was just plain mad too. "It's not stealing if they're my chickens."

He shrugged. "Look, I'll show you where they are. You can figure out the rest when you go back again. No one expects you to know anything, since you just moved here, but everyone knows I know better." He looked at the wagon. "Leave it here, and I'll show you; if not, I'm going home. I have to get ready for the poultry show."

Whether he had a point or not, I did need his help. Otherwise, I'd have to ask for directions, and someone was sure to remember that later. I knew in my heart I was right and that I had to get the chickens back as quickly as I could. But I still didn't really want to discuss chicken stealing with my mom either.

If I was going to have to make two long bike rides before dinner, I'd better get moving. "Fine. Let's go."

Chris took off down the road, and I pedaled hard to keep up.

I like to ride my bike fast, but I didn't know my way very well, and Chris's legs are longer than mine. For the first while, I had to work to keep up, and to try and keep track of which road we went down, since they all looked the same to me, and I was going to have to come back alone.

I guess it's pretty around here—everything looks like those paintings that are just scenery, with nothing actually happening. I saw a few sheep on one farm, but they weren't doing anything interesting, just chewing grass. It was hot, so I don't really blame them, but it was still boring.

And so, even though I was scared of the hawk-chicken and Ms. Griegson, and I was still riding my bike as fast as I could to keep up with Chris, I started thinking. I thought about how I was going to explain three more chickens to my parents, especially since I wasn't going to ask permission first. I thought about what my parents would say when Ms. Griegson turned up again and told them now I was stealing her chickens off her farm, and made it sound all reasonable to give them back to her. I didn't have any good ideas for any of it, really. I wondered what was special about these chickens, and if I'd be able to figure it out myself, or if it was something I couldn't really know until later, like Buffy's chicks. It was kind of too bad, I thought, that I didn't have at least one of her chicks left to turn that hawk-chicken to stone. But you really can't treat a chick or even a baby cockatrice like a weapon, just pulling it out when you want to. And I guess it isn't really the hawk-chicken's fault either. It's a creature too, and it has its own things it needs, and it should be able to peck around and scratch for bugs and do whatever it likes doing, at least most of the time. But I don't want hawk-chicks that can turn things to stone, or make things float, or disappear, or even run fast.

Chris looked back, and then he stopped for a moment. I thought he was just waiting for me to catch up, and to tell you the truth, I was too tired to even be really mad about it. But when I puffed my way up to him, he pointed up in the air, back the way we came. There was a hawk circling.

I had a bad moment then. I knew I hadn't put the chickens in the henhouse before I left. (Not that

Henrietta wouldn't just let them right out again if she felt like it.) I knew they were smart chickens, and special, but what would that do against a hawk? Even a regular one?

I wanted to go home right then and there. But Chris was waiting on me, and really, it would take me so long to get back, what could I do for them now? Meanwhile, three more chickens needed my help, and I wouldn't be able to find my way on my own.

I took a deep breath and told Chris, "Let's keep going."

He nodded, and started pedaling again, maybe a tiny bit slower this time. I hate feeling like I can never catch up.

I tried to distract myself by thinking up a plan. I didn't know how long Ms. Griegson would be setting up for the show, so I'd need to ask Chris about that. I didn't know much about the hawk—I really wished I'd asked you more about that. All I could think of was luring the chickens into the dog crate. (I know, I really ought to wash it first, and put something in the bottom, only what? I don't have any wood shavings.) And pulling the crate in the wagon home. Which seemed like an awfully slow and noisy escape for a chicken thief. I was starting to see Chris's point, but even though he's guessed there's something unusual about Great-Uncle Jim's chickens, he doesn't know how special they really are, or why I can't let Ms. Griegson keep them. Not to mention that every time I imagined pulling the wagonload home, I imagined that hawk picking up the crate and carrying it off. What could I do to stop it if it tried?

Suddenly Chris glanced back. He pulled off the road, over the bump at the edge, and down into a ditch.

I followed. What else could I do? I wasn't so graceful, though; I fell off my bike at the bottom and ended up sprawled in the dirt as Chris crouched down behind a group of thistles.

Then I heard a truck. I looked up; I couldn't help myself. It was the orange pickup. Ms. Griegson looked straight ahead, so I don't think she saw us. But I couldn't see what was in the back of the truck.

I squinted down the road. No sign of the hawk. Should I tell Chris about Ms. Griegson's hawk-chicken?

But when I looked back at him, he was already pushing his bike in the opposite direction. I ran after him, my bike left in the dust. "Hey!"

He didn't look at me. "Just keep going down the hill. There's a split-rail fence at the bottom, where the trees are. Past them you'll see the chicken coop in the field. I have to get home."

I was pretty mad at him then, but what could I do? I thought he agreed they were my chickens, not Ms. Griegson's. I thought he wanted to help me. But you can't really make someone do the right thing, or help you when you need help. Just like you can't make someone trust you, or be your friend.

So I walked back to my bike. By the time I pushed it up onto the road, he was out of sight, off around the curve in the road. Maybe he was just scared. I was pretty scared too.

I kept on riding, more slowly now, and I kept a sharp ear out for that orange pickup. But I didn't hear anything, and I didn't see any driveways before I got to the bottom of the hill and the fence Chris told me about. I pulled my bike behind a big bush and leaned it up against the fence, and I took a good look through the row of trees at the chicken coop.

It looked like a wood shack maybe thirty feet away, on the other side of the fence. I could see that the windows were covered in chicken wire. I couldn't see any chickens around, and I was nervous about that. I hate to admit it, because I really have tried to study, but I couldn't remember what a Speckled Sussex looks like. I think it's because even though I've looked at a lot of pictures in a lot of chicken books, I haven't really seen that many chickens myself, at least not to know what kind they are. So I decided since Chris had run away anyway, I might as well go have a look and make sure I could tell which ones were mine, just in case Ms. Griegson had been stealing other people's chickens too. I really wasn't going to have much luck explaining all this if I stole the wrong chickens.

Then I heard an engine start up. I ducked back

behind the bush with my bike, and just in time, because the orange pickup came right back down the road. I had a bad feeling about that. But not the kind of bad feeling that meant I could just go home.

I was careful to have a good look around all the trees and high up in the sky before I slipped under the fence. But I could still feel my shoulders hunched almost up to my ears as I walked across the short grass toward the shed. What would those hawk claws feel like if it found me here?

But I made it to the shed, and ducked under the short eave. Ms. Griegson was pretty sure of herself; it wasn't locked or anything. Then again, no one would believe me in a case of her word against mine.

Peering through the window, I could see three chickens I didn't know in the shed, brown with white-and-black speckles, and then I held my breath. Four chickens I knew very well were there too. Ms. Griegson had stolen all of my chickens.

I stared and stared at them. I'd seen them all when I fed them earlier, before Chris came over, so she must have just brought them here. I felt so mad at her then, but also so useless. I was only gone for an hour or so, and she just drove right up and stole my chickens, and no one stopped her. What was I supposed to do now?

Then Henrietta noticed me at the window. She hopped down from her perch and clucked her way over to the floor below the window, clucking louder and louder. The other chickens hopped down too and hurried along behind.

I glanced around. I still couldn't see anyone, but someone was going to notice all this racket pretty soon.

The door latch rattled. Henrietta didn't know this kind, but that didn't stop her from trying. It was clear she wanted out.

I shivered. The chickens didn't seem to mind, but I didn't want to leave them in that dark shed. I looked at the chicken wire on the window. It didn't seem all that sturdy. But I didn't have any way to get them home safely, and there were hawks around, even if Ms. Griegson had really gone off to the poultry show this time.

The door latch rattled again, and this time the hook just kept on rattling until it worked its way out of the loop and fell hanging. The door opened. Henrietta glared at me.

The hens spilled out of the doorway and started pecking at the grass with little chortles of glee.

I don't need a lecture that stealing is wrong, or that I should never break into anyone's farm buildings. I know that already. (Better than Ms. Griegson, apparently.) And I know that letting Henrietta open the door and let all the chickens out without even trying to put them back in is just as bad. But what can I say? I decided right then that if

I had to do the wrong thing to keep my chickens safe and bring them home, that's what I was going to do. I didn't know chicken keeping was going to be this complicated, but that's how it is, I guess, at least with unusual chickens.

The chickens followed me quickly enough, as soon as I gave them some sunflower seeds, and when I started jogging back toward the road, they ran along behind me across the field, flapping their wings for little bursts of speed on their drumstick legs.

I swear I could feel it before I looked up and saw it. A shadow went over me, and there was a big rush of wind, and a huge bird flew back up into the sky as I ducked. So I ran for the trees along Ms. Griegson's fence, waving my arms and yelling, as though that could somehow save my chickens. Then I felt that rush of wind again. I wish I could tell you exactly what it looked like, but I was so scared I closed my eyes. I'm not very proud of that, but it's the truth. Then I remembered the chickens, and I snapped my eyes open, just as it soared up.

I counted six, all huddled in a little group, with Henrietta and Buffy staring up after the hawk. I counted six again, only six, and I felt like a huge lightning storm was going to explode out of my chest, and I tried to remember whether I'd seen the hawk carrying anything as it flew away. But then Chameleon slowly unfaded back into view, and I could start panting again, trying to catch up on breathing. Then I remembered we still weren't safe, and started running again, making sure they followed.

This time Roadrunner ran ahead into the trees, far faster than I could, and I wasn't too sure whether Henrietta's feet were touching the ground. Buffy was the slowest; she's not built for speed. So, when the hawk dove again, Buffy was last of the group, and when she saw it, she stopped altogether.

I thought maybe she got frozen with fear, the way people say they do when they get mugged. But she was glaring and glaring at that hawk, and I looked at it, and you know, it looked kind of frozen too. Then suddenly it was shooting off in a different direction, not flapping, and I looked around, and Henrietta was glaring at it too.

I don't know if she really likes Buffy much, but she doesn't want anyone else being top chicken, that's for sure. It's a good thing she knows that with great power comes great responsibility. Not like that hawk-chicken.

We ran some more. We made it to the trees, and through the fence, and to my bike. I couldn't see the hawk, but I was pretty sure Buffy didn't turn it to stone.

I gave them each a few seeds as a reward. Then I looked at my bike, looked at the chickens, and wondered what on earth I was going to do now.

I was already past sensible, I knew that. Which also

meant I was past asking anyone for help (since I was breaking the law, or at least common sense and good manners). My cell phone had no service, of course, not that it ever does around here, and not that there was anyone I could call. And even special chickens—or maybe especially special chickens—can't be left on their own by the side of the road for an hour without any sort of box or anything.

And then I felt that shadow again, and the chickens started to run, and I ran after them, flapping my arms and yelling to keep that hawk away.

It didn't seem strange to me at the time, what with everything going on, but the chickens knew where they were going. They ran up the driveway next door, around the corner, and into a barn that was open just a crack, and I ran after them, slamming the door behind me as soon as I counted seven chickens.

It was dark in the barn, except for a little bit of light from the high dusty windows, but I didn't care. I just breathed until my lungs caught up with my heart and everything calmed down.

One of the Speckled Sussex went over to a pile of wood shavings in a corner, sat down, and started fluffing up her feathers. Then the others joined in, all fluffing and rolling around, looking like their bones had melted away, like jellyfish chickens, clouds of dust everywhere, clucking their contentment.

I didn't know what to do. I was stuck in a stranger's barn with seven loose chickens that no one knew were mine, and a hawk-chicken outside.

I stared at the barn wall for a while, and blinked and blinked, trying to pretend everything would be okay. Then I got out my cell phone and had a look. One bar, then nothing, then one bar again, just for a second. I tried calling my parents over and over, while the chickens rolled around in the dust. I was desperate for Mom or Dad to come pick us up, and also scared the call would go through and they'd answer. But it didn't.

Then came part of my day I'd rather not tell you about. I know I'm old enough to be responsible for my actions and not to lose it like a two-year-old, but I know that even my dad cried when he got laid off, and once in a while after that when he thought no one was looking. I know my mom can swear a blue streak in two languages when she thinks I'm somewhere else and things aren't going so well, like when her computer died and the rent was due and even my cousin Javier (who's really good at that stuff and works for UCLA's computer labs now) couldn't fix it. So let's just say I'm not proud of how I acted, and I'm sure I wasted some time, but I really couldn't think what else to do.

Finally, I realized I was blinking at a sign on the wall: REDWOOD FARM SUPPLY, just over a wooden desk and a big filing cabinet.

I took a deep breath and said, "Agnes, I'm really sorry about your chickens." I don't really know why I felt like I had to tell you. I didn't like the way my voice was trembling, and I hated saying the words at all; it felt like admitting I had really screwed up. And even though I had, I didn't want to go on about it. But it was like the words needed to get out, like if I didn't let them out of my mouth, they were going to claw their way out of my chest like an alien or something. "I thought I could get them home safe, but I can't, and now I don't know what to do." Then my eyes blurred for a while, and the pressure in my chest lifted just enough that I could swallow down the rest of the words and keep them to myself a little longer.

When I looked up, the hens were clustered near the door, squawking to get out. "Hush," I told them, a little desperately.

But of course Henrietta didn't listen. She's getting really good at door latches.

The chickens all ran out before I could stop them, and I ran after them, waving my arms and looking for the hawk. But I didn't see it.

Instead, I saw a house, and what looked like it was probably a vegetable garden before the weeds took over, and some fields that didn't really have anything in them that I could tell, and the barn I'd just come out of. I'm sorry to have to tell you this, Agnes, but your farm looks really run-down, like those paintings of barns with the

roof falling in. Not quite that bad, but you know. I'm
sorry.

I forgot to watch the chickens for a minute, I was so
startled. Then I realized that things like that don't just
happen overnight, or even in a couple of weeks, so it
couldn't have all been ruined since I'd stopped hearing
from you. And then I remembered Señora Gilberto's
house, which looked like an absolute wreck ever since
her son died, but she still lived there anyway, even
if it did freak people out who walked by and saw her
rocking on a porch where the steps and railing had
fallen off.

I didn't know what to think. I yelled for you too,
Agnes, but you didn't come. I don't know how long I
yelled. Nothing moved on your farm. Nothing looked like
it had moved for a long time.

Suddenly I heard a car coming around the curve,
and I yelled for the chickens to get back in the barn,
which worked about as well as you'd expect, chickens not
being really good at obedience-school kinds of things,
as far as I know, and never having been trained. I threw
the sunflower seeds I was clutching, and that worked a
little better, and I ran after them. The car pulled around
the corner, and I looked up, terrified it would be Ms.
Griegson.

But it was Gregory, delivering the mail. "Hello,
Sophie," he said, smiling. "Nice chickens."

"Hi, Gregory," I said automatically. I looked at the chickens. "Thanks." It was like my brain just stopped working. I couldn't think of a single excuse for why I'd be out with seven chickens on a farm that looked—I'm sorry to say this—like it had been abandoned. Which made me realize I had a question. "Gregory, do you deliver my letters to Agnes here?"

"Yes, I sure do," he said, looking more serious now. "Through rain, and sleet, and snow, and sometimes some pretty hot days with no air-conditioning." He pushed the barn door open and walked over to a box on the desk in there marked OUTBOX. There was nothing in there. He looked at the blank paper in the typewriter on the desk and sighed.

"Why doesn't she write back anymore?" I asked. I don't know why I thought he'd know something like that.

"Well . . . I don't know the answer to that, not for sure."

When I looked up, he was watching my chickens. "Looks like maybe you might want to mail your chickens to the poultry show? Or are your parents on their way?"

I couldn't help it then; I started to cry. I sat right down on the barn floor and cried hard.

Gregory patted my shoulder. He went out and got a flat piece of cardboard and folded it up into a box, sticking a big piece of tape on the bottom. Then he put it down and whistled.

The chickens ignored him. So I got slowly back up again and threw the last few sunflower seeds into the box.

Henrietta was first; she jumped right in. Buffy followed, and slowly, so did my others. The Speckled Sussex were last. They looked around anxiously for a moment, and then jumped in too. Gregory folded the lid down right away. He looked at me.

I gave a big sniff and a big gulp. "Thanks. But I think maybe we should just go home. Only, I don't have any money for postage."

Gregory hesitated. "I'm sorry, Sophie, but I've already been by your farm; I can't go back that way without delaying my route. I can take your chickens to the show, or I can give your parents a call when I get back to the post office and they can pick you all up. What's your pick?"

My heart, which had been sort of soggy and sad with all that crying (really, I almost never cry normally, honest), started pounding and pounding again. I walked over to the doorway and checked the sky; still clear, but for how long? But Ms. Griegson was sure to be at the poultry show. "Gregory, speaking purely hypothetically, how would you keep your chickens safe if someone wanted to steal them from you?" ("Purely hypothetically" is what my mom always says when she asks how you would murder someone, or hide the body.

It's so you don't worry. I don't think it always works with people who don't know she's working on a mystery novel as well as her articles.)

One thing I like about Gregory is that he puts a lot of thought in before he answers you. "Purely hypothetically," he said, "I would want to make sure everyone who knew poultry in this town knew they were mine. So no one could claim there was a mistake. So I'd take them to the poultry show."

"Even if they were, hypothetically, a little unusual? And even if you hadn't paid a fee and sent in a form by the deadline and didn't have any money?" I asked. I wasn't feeling any less anxious.

"Registration forms and fees are just for judging," he said. "You can still be part of the show-and-tell area; you just can't win any awards." He rubbed his beard for a moment. "How about we do this, then: I'll pay for your postage, and help you get set up at the show as soon as I finish my route. In return, you can bring me a dozen eggs when these girls are home laying again."

I had to think hard about that. What I really wanted most of all was to shut them all up in the henhouse until I knew it was safe for them to come out again. But Gregory was right: it wasn't going to be safe until everyone knew they were mine, not Ms. Griegson's. "Do I have to do an oral presentation?" (I really hate talking in front of a class.)

Gregory nodded, serious. "You'll need to tell everyone what breeds of chicken they are, and how long you've had them, and all that."

That was another problem. "What if they don't believe me?" I asked. My voice was really small.

But Gregory still heard me. He sighed. "Sometimes people don't believe the truth even when it's in front of them," he said. "Sometimes you just have to do the best you can to explain it to them."

I sure hoped I didn't have to explain the parts about Henrietta using the Force and all the rest to everyone too. Which reminded me—that egg bargain sounded good, but it was kind of tricky too, since there are all the rules about refrigerating and the glass eggs and who knew what the Speckled Sussex would lay. But it was that or have my parents come, who-knows-how-long later, to pick me up with three chickens they didn't know I had. So I decided I'd just have to work the eggs out somehow. "Deal," I said. "Only, it might take a few weeks to collect them all, and some of the eggs might have a little bit of sand in them."

He laughed. "I'm used to it. I got my eggs from Agnes Taylor for years."

"But not now?" I asked, pretty anxious.

"Not recently, no," he said. Then he picked up the box and carried it to the mail truck, the chickens squawking. He looked around. "That your bike over there?"

I nodded.

"I can't carry passengers in my truck, and you shouldn't be getting in any cars unless your parents know, anyways," he said. "You going to be able to get to the show okay?"

I hesitated. I really didn't want to go anywhere near Ms. Griegson's farm. "Will you wait just a minute while I grab my bike?"

Gregory nodded. He waited until I ran back, pushing my bike. Then he got into his mail truck. "See you there," he said.

"Thanks, Gregory. Don't leave my chickens alone, though, okay?"

"You got it. See you there soon," he said, and started up the truck.

It was a good thing Gregory had to make lots of stops to deliver mail, because I had a hard time keeping up. But I managed to get there when he did. Gregory helped carry the box in to get the chickens set up, and he found a phone where I could call my parents and explain where I was, and ask if they could come pick me up later. I didn't explain about the chickens. Someone else needed to use the phone.

The chickens were pretty mad at me. Chickens are not very quiet when they're mad. But they waited in the show's wire cage (they had to share a big one, since the show people didn't know we were coming).

I'm still wondering, Agnes—did you move? Is that why you don't write back anymore? Why didn't you tell Gregory where to forward your mail?

Sophie

Blackbird Farm

July 1, 2014 (later)

Agnes
Redwood Farm Supply
Gravenstein, CA 95472

Dear Agnes,

I guess you probably already know how poultry shows
work, but I didn't. What happens here, at least, is that
there's a big room with a lot of wire cages in it, all
different sizes for different kinds of poultry. There's
an area for the show part, where the judging happens,
where you pay money and might win ribbons, and
that's very quiet and you feel like you should tiptoe and
whisper. (Well, aside from the chickens and ducks and
all that. Chickens and ducks are never quiet. Emus are
usually pretty quiet, though, it turns out, except when
they make a weird gurgly booming noise.)

Then there's the other half of the room, where I
was, which is mostly kids (and chickens and ducks and
turkeys and geese and I think maybe quail and also
one ostrich), where nobody is very quiet at all. (Except
maybe the quail, and sometimes the ostrich. But the
ostrich boomed sometimes too; it's related to the emu.)

186

As soon as kids started coming in to set up, I could see they all knew each other, and a lot of them had fancy signs about their chickens, and even decorations for their cages and stuff. My stomach felt pretty bad, and I'd had a really long day, and I really didn't want to talk about any of it.

I decided Ms. Griegson probably couldn't steal my chickens in front of everybody, and I didn't see her around anyway. And my chickens were all fluffed up together having naps, not doing anything unusual, and no one was paying any attention to them with an ostrich and everything here. So I walked around and looked at all the poultry. I don't know what makes a chicken win a ribbon or not. Maybe good behavior? I was kind of relieved my chickens were not in the part for awards, even if they were pretty tired out from their adventures. They're not really obedient.

I saw Ms. Griegson's Rhode Island Reds. I mean, the ones she brought, not all of them. I don't know if the one that chased us is the only one that turns into a hawk. None of them turned into anything else at the show, at least not while I was watching.

When I finished walking around the room, I saw that Chris was setting up. He looked sort of nervous when he saw me, so I told him my chickens were fine now. He bit his lip and looked at his sneakers. "Want to see my surprise?" he asked, like he thought I might say no.

But I said sure. I was too tired and nervous to be mad.

He had six chicks that looked like they had fluffy hats on, with a special red light and everything to keep them warm. They're a kind called Polish chickens, that get fancy hairdos when they're older. (Feather-dos? Fluffy feathers on their heads. Like wigs.) I guess his mom must have felt bad about what happened to Buffy's chicks. He was pretty proud of his new chicks, and lots of kids came by to see them, but I think he only let me hold them. They are the softest, fluffiest things ever, like pom-poms, even if they do poop on your hands sometimes. (I love my chickens best, of course. But his were really cute. [I think they're only regular-unusual, though, not super-unusual. I watched them pretty carefully, and I think I would have noticed.])

Then the presentations started, and my stomach felt a whole lot worse. I really, really don't like talking in front of people. Ms. O'Malley asked for volunteers, and an older girl's hand shot up. I listened for a little bit. I never knew someone could know so much about regular old geese.

My stomach wasn't feeling any better, so I went to find Gregory. I borrowed some paper and a pen from him so I could make notes. Ever since that time when I couldn't remember a single thing about Benjamin Franklin and almost cried in front of the whole third grade from embarrassment, I always write notes.

When I walked back to where my chickens were, Ms. Griegson was standing in front of their cage, looking at them. You know, she still didn't really look like a mean lady. She looked kind of sad. And if she'd just asked me when I first found them, I might even have let her have my chickens. I bet she's better at taking care of them than me.

But those are not her chickens, not even if she really wants them. So just taking them isn't fair. I've thought about it a lot, and she just can't go around breeding dangerous unknown superchicken mixes that will have to get killed like Buffy's chicks. I have enough problems these days keeping my chickens safe, and I've seen those superhero movies. I don't need the army and SWAT teams after my chickens too.

When she saw me, she crossed her arms, but she didn't move away from my chickens. So when Ms. O'Malley asked for the next volunteer, even though my stomach was turning over and over like on that spinning ride that my cousin Javier threw up on, I raised my hand.

Chris raised his hand too. He looked really excited to talk about his chicks. Ms. O'Malley called on him. But he looked over at me, putting my hand down, and he saw Ms. Griegson standing near my chickens, and he said, "Sophie can go next. I'll go after her."

Then everybody looked at me. I said, "Hello, I'm

Sophie Brown," but my voice was quiet and squeaky and shaky all at once, and I thought for a minute about just turning and leaving. But Gregory gave me a big nod, just like my teacher Mr. Hightower at my science fair in LA. I lived through that. And my parents had arrived too, and they smiled at me. So I took a deep breath and looked down at my notes, like Mr. Hightower taught me. Here's what I said:

"Hello, I'm Sophie Brown. These are the chickens I inherited from my great-uncle, Jim Brown, when he died. That's why they might look familiar. Henrietta is a bantam White Leghorn. Chameleon is a Barred Rock. Roadrunner is a bantam Black Frizzle Cochin." (Ms. O'Malley said, "KO-chin, Sophie, not ko-CHIN," really loudly, and Mom glared at her. I got confused for a minute and lost my place in my notes. Then I found my place again and kept going.) "Buffy is a Buff Orpington. And these three are Speckled Sussex. I'm not sure what their names are yet. They are all laying hens."

I took a quick glance at the chickens. They were still just sitting there, thank goodness. I don't know what I would have done if Henrietta had gotten mad.

Then I looked at the crowd. Gregory nodded again, and my mom waved, and my dad gave me a big thumbs-up. But Ms. Griegson was still there, with her arms crossed, just looking at me and my chickens, waiting.

One thing both my parents agree on is this: if people

are doing something unfair, it's part of our job to remind them what's fair, even if sometimes it still doesn't turn out the way we want it to.

So I looked up at all those farm people and kids I don't know yet, and I swallowed down my wriggly stomach, and I said, "Now that you know that these are my chickens, will you help me watch over them? It seems like someone has been trying to steal them."

I didn't look at Ms. Griegson. I know people would rather believe the person they know than the person they don't know. Especially if the person they don't know is just a kid.

But everyone else looked at her. I don't know if it was because she's in charge of the poultry show, or because Ms. O'Malley was glaring at her. I was kind of worried that my parents would say something, but they just looked at her too.

Ms. Griegson got pretty still. "That's a very serious thing to say, Sophie. I know you're new here, and my guess is there's been a mistake. We can talk more about it after the show." She turned to Chris, and everyone else looked at him too. "Your turn, Chris."

But Chris was still looking at me. "If there's a chicken thief in the area, I think we should hear about it," he said. And, you know, I forgave him right then for riding off and leaving me earlier. Sometimes people just need a little time to figure out what's right.

"Exactly what I was going to say!" said Ms. O'Malley loudly. "Sophie is not the kind of girl who makes things up."

And everyone looked back at me, even Ms. Griegson.

So I took a deep breath, and I kept going, even though I didn't have notes about this part. "I think you all know that Great-Uncle Jim had unusual chickens. They've been finding their way home to our farm, so now I'm taking care of them. I'd really appreciate it if you'd help me keep them safe."

I've never heard a pin drop, but I bet I could have heard one then if there was one around that happened to be dropping. People stopped looking at me, but they sure looked at my chickens. (Well, all except my parents, who looked pretty confused.) Everyone waited. I think they guessed what I meant by unusual, even if they didn't exactly know all the details, and even if no one ever talks about it.

After a minute, Ms. Griegson uncrossed her arms and smiled at me. "Sophie, I'm certain you're learning all you can, but you're very new to farming, and these are not exactly beginner's chickens. Jim Brown was a poultry expert. If they're getting away from you already, perhaps the best way we can help you keep them safe is by taking care of them while you start with a nice easy breed. I'm sure we could find you some beautiful Comet chicks."

I didn't trust my voice not to shake, so I put my hand on top of the wire cage with my chickens in it and I shook my head. The Speckled Sussex were distracting me, huddled at one end and clucking. I hoped they weren't going to do anything unusual that I couldn't handle right then. Before I could really think about it, I opened my mouth and said, "Agnes said they were mine. She told me not to give them to anyone."

So much for pins dropping. It was like wind rushed through a noisy tree in fall, every leaf muttering something to its neighbor. Every one except Ms. Griegson, who put her hand on my chickens' cage too. "But how . . ."

Without taking my eyes off her, I told the crowd, "I know these chickens are a big responsibility. That's why I need you all to help me. Will you help me keep them safe?"

"Of course I will," Ms. O'Malley said at once.

"Yes!" shouted Chris.

And Gregory nodded. And my parents looked confused, but they nodded too. And I saw that girl with the llama book, and she was nodding, and so was Jane from the feedstore, and the black lady in the business suit standing next to her smiled and nodded at me. And all around the room, all those people I'd seen in town but don't really know started nodding too.

And then they all looked at Ms. Griegson.

I couldn't help but stare at her too. I just waited, and I wouldn't look away. I'm not an expert like my mom is, but I guess I'm still better at waiting than Ms. Griegson. Everyone else quieted down eventually and they waited too.

Finally, she looked up from my chickens. She took her hand off their cage and looked out at all those people who were looking at her and waiting. Then she took a step back and said, "Of course, we would never tolerate a chicken thief in our community. Sophie, thank you for alerting us. Everyone, please let me know immediately if you see any signs of theft, or any poultry go missing." And she took three more steps away from my chickens and joined the crowd.

There was a gust of wind through the room, and my chickens made a racket when it blew through their cage. Then they settled down, even the Speckled Sussex, and went back to sleep.

I was so relieved, I kind of wanted to throw up. My stomach had really been through a lot today.

But I thanked everyone, even Ms. Griegson, and my parents started to clap really loudly, and Ms. Griegson hurried over to Chris's chicks and told him to go ahead. But he waited until everyone finished clapping for me before he started.

A lot of people came up to me later and told me how good it was to see Jim Brown's chickens at a show again, and what a loss his death was to the community. I didn't know what to say, so I just said thank you.

I met a nice reporter named Joy who was doing an article for the paper on the poultry show. She took a picture of me with my chickens, and she said she'd put it in the paper so everyone will know they're mine. She speaks Spanish, but she's not from LA or Mexico; she's Filipina. But it was still nice to hear some Spanish again. I told her my mom is a writer too, and I saw them talking together later. Maybe Mom will get to write about poultry shows too one day, and she'll take me with her when she goes to cover the story, like she used to sometimes.

Ms. O'Malley introduced me to lots of other adult chicken people who arrived later as "Jim Brown's grandniece, who inherited his chickens and his good poultry sense." I think she said this extra loud when Ms. Griegson was nearby, which I guess was nice of her. Apparently, she doesn't really get along all that well with Ms. Griegson. When people looked at me all surprised, she'd add in a loud whisper, "Sophie's mother is from Mexico." I gave up trying to explain that really Mom's from LA. Whatever. People will work it all out for themselves eventually.

I was glad my parents came, though. And I was really relieved they didn't say anything about the three extra chickens. They aren't really chicken people yet, so maybe they didn't notice? Or maybe they just guessed I'd had kind of a hard day. But they both said I did a really good job, and that they were proud of me, and that my voice hardly shook at all. Neither of them said one word to Ms. Griegson.

Dad had a really good time talking to everyone— I guess I hadn't realized he was kind of lonely too. Jane from the feedstore came up and gave me a big hug and told me I did great, and introduced us to her girlfriend, Violet, who was still in her city work clothes. Violet told Dad some of the tricks Great-Uncle Jim used to run the farm by himself. Like that thing that isn't a tractor— it's a harvester. Dad said maybe I could drive it too if Mom said it was okay, after Violet teaches him how to work it.

Chris introduced me to some of the other kids. Some of them had some nice-looking chickens. And the girl with the llama book really does have a llama, a brown one. The girl's name is Samantha, and her llama's name is Ella. Did you know some people have guard llamas for their sheep? Samantha wasn't sure if Ella would know how to guard against chicken thieves, but she said if I have any more trouble to let her know and she would look it up in her book. (She didn't bring Ella to the poultry show, though, because llamas are not poultry. Obviously.) I guess I'll talk to them more when I start school in the fall. And Gregory stayed through the whole thing too. Did you know Gregory raises Call ducks? They're cute, but man, are they loud. And he asked for my recipe for migas. I know Gregory will love migas.

Agnes, I'm not quite sure how to ask you this, but are you dead? I mean, I don't think that's a very polite question under normal circumstances, but I heard a guy telling someone else something about "before old Miss Taylor died," and he gave me a funny look. It gave me quite a turn, just like my grandmother always said, so I didn't ask him about it.

If you are dead, I guess I don't expect you to answer. But, well, I don't know. I'm not even sure why I keep writing to you. It seems like you would want to know. But maybe not anymore.

> Your friend forever,
> Sophie

PS I guess it's okay if you can't send me lessons anymore. I'll keep getting books from the library. And Gregory said maybe he'd even start another 4-H poultry club on a different day, since the other one is pretty full, and there might be kids that can't go on Wednesday evenings. He mostly knows about ducks, but I guess he could read up on chickens.

PPS Why do you think the Speckled Sussex keep

following me into the barn and then going up in the loft? It's a real pain to get them down the ladder, I tell you, and I don't want them making a mess up here. But don't worry, they're all back where they belong, and nobody got hurt.

My name is...uh... Sophie Brown... ...ah...

GRAVENSTEIN INDEPENDENT JOURNAL

July 2, 2014

Sophie Brown, 12, carrying on her great-uncle Jim Brown's chicken-farming tradition

NOTE: Ms. Brown alerted the community to a poultry thief in the area. Citizens are encouraged to report any suspicious behavior to the Rural Crime Prevention Unit as well as notifying the poultry association president and vice president. Help keep our farms safe!

POULTRY SHOW ENCOURAGES KIDS TO FARM

by Joy Ocampo

Young poultry farmers were encouraged to bring their birds to the Gravenstein Poultry Show this year, and over 15 young people (ages 5 to 18) participated. Community events such as these encourage kids to value farm life, says Mayor

Continued on p. 12

Blackbird Farm

July 5, 2014

Agnes Taylor (I think?)
Redwood Farm Supply
Gravenstein, CA 95472

Dear Agnes,

I think I'm starting to understand it now. The Speckled
Sussex finally found what they were looking for—the
old typewriter I have in the loft. They kept pecking and
pecking at the keys, until finally I put some more paper
in it to show them how it's done.

I typed "The quick brown fox jumps over the lazy
dog" like Mom taught me, to check that they hadn't
messed up the keys, and then a little bit of !&$?! for
emphasis. I left the paper in the typewriter and got them
all back down again.

But later this afternoon, I saw the barn door had
swung open again, so I went back up and found them.
And this letter was in the typewriter. So I read it.

Thanks for letting me know.

Your friend,
Sophie

The quick brown fox jumps over the lazy dog !&$?!()
()%!!!

ddear sophie,.,.,.

iii'm afraid i am dead. don''tt bother askiing me about
what itt''s like after death or any of that.,.,, there was
a sharp pain one day, 777a7nd then things got pretty
blurry for a while, 7an7d then gregory came into the
barn saying i had mail. and when i tried to pick it up, my
hands went right through it.

sory about tthe delay in answeriing yourletters;'l';
it took me abit to train the sspeckled sussex. they can't
do capitals 77an7d sometimes they peck the wrong
keys.,.,bother.,. in case you haven't guessed, they can
see ghosts,.,.,, so i can show them which keys to hit.bbut
they don't usually type, and they aren'''t any better at
understanding ghost-=people than any other chicken.
so it's a slow process, typing. and aii couldn't write at all
after they'd been taken away.

asdaabbout sue griegson.,, sue used to work for me..
iit'ss not so much that she is a bad person as that she
makes bad decisions. shhe shouuld never have stolen
your chickens, nno matter how much she wanted
them,.,., you know that. she doesn't.

ytyou've done brilliantly. ii had no idea you'd have
such a time of it, nor thatyou'd manage so well. i'm going
to try and get the sussex to write a few more letters for

you, to make things easier. but, sophie, i'm not sure i'll be here much longer. iffeel faded around the edges, 777and like i've finished things up. maybe i'll have that next adventure after all.

woulld you please pput a fresh sheet of paper in the tytuypewriter when you can? then please maiil the letter tto the address atthe top when it";s done. thank you.

your friend.,.,alwys
aagnes

p.s. jijim says he's so proud of you, 77a7nd thanks for taking care of the chickens. allso, tell your dad the bird netting"s in the back of the loft 777and7 to put it on right away if he wants any grapes this year.

p.pp thee oter lessonsare in the file cabinet in my barn. gregory can show you. you have my permission. and pls tell gregory thnks.

messrs. dougherty
1010 sunnyside dr.
santa rosa, ca 95405

dear messrs. dougherty,

i, agnes taylor, do leave to miss sophie brown the
remainder of my poultry business, formerly known
as redwood farm, including all my remaining poultry
currently held by other keepers. it will need to be held
for her until she comes of legal age by her parents, who
seem to have pretty good sense for non-poultry people.
however, they cannot sell it or give it away; it must be
held for her until such time as she herself comes of age
and decides what to do with it.

   also, please send that letter you have on file to the list
of addresses we discussed. i know you may be somewhat
surprised to receive this missive from me at this point,
but that was how i wished it to be done. surely you must
agree it will be easiest for all concerned to just follow my
instructions.

                        sincerely,
                        agnes taylor

ps in case you do not believe this is really me, i conclude
with the following: mr. thornton dougherty tried to kiss
me in the barn when we were twelve, and i punched him
in the eye. i never told anyone, and i suspect he never did
either, since the rumor was he'd been hit by a barn shutter.

Agnes Taylor
Wherever you are now

Dear Agnes,

I wanted you to know that it's okay if you can't stay. I guess no one can stay forever. I have a lot of questions for you still, but maybe they'll just keep being part of the mystery.

I mailed your letter like you asked me to, and today a big fancy letter came to me on the kind of paper my mom says is a huge waste of money, saying I'd inherited your business. My parents were pretty surprised. I don't really want to know what Ms. Griegson will say.

Gregory's going to come over later and take me for a tour, since he had a key to take care of your chickens and knows them pretty well. I think that's very nice of him. I appreciate it that he didn't try to explain you were dead. I feel like Gregory is the kind of person who understands that life's just more mysterious than most people think, and is okay with leaving it like that. I'm going to try and be like that too.

So, all I want to say is, thank you.

Your friend forever,
Sophie

PS I may not be an exceptional poultry farmer just yet. But I promise I will try to learn everything I can so I can become one soon.

PPS I asked Gregory if he had any tips on how to be an exceptional poultry farmer. He gave me a big nod, and said he thought I was doing just fine. I do like Gregory.

PPPS If you ever do meet my grandmother, wherever you go, would you please tell her I love her very much? And that I'm doing fine?

SOPHIE'S TO-DO'S:

Read at least one book this week

Help cook dinner

Dry dishes

Clean room

Take out trash, recycling & compost

Sort out some of Great-Uncle Jim's junk

Take library books back

Feed & water chickens

Clean out henhouse

Try Gregory's recipe for egg & cheese sandwiches

Tour Redwood Farm with Gregory

Work on comics with Chris

Meet Ella (Samantha's llama)

Talk to Dad about getting a guard llama

DAD'S TO-DO'S:

Learn how to drive the tractor & harvester

Put bird netting on grapes

Ask Violet or Gregory what other summer chores need to be done

Make appointment with viticulture farm adviser

Sign up for viticulture course

Consult with Sophie about poultry farming

Build third rope swing

Cook dinner

Wash dishes

Clean bathroom & kitchen

MOM'S TO-DO'S:

Write "Coming Back to Farm Life: An Essay" (due 7/14)

Write "10 Reasons to Take Your Kids to a Farm" (due 7/15)

Write "A Brief History of Migas in America" (due 7/16)

Write "Regaining Your Culture Through Recipes" (due 7/16)

Write "Decorating for Fall with Farm Tools" (due 7/17)

Write "Are Chickens Right for You and Your Family?" (due 7/18)

Talk to Joy about covering the tractor show while she's on vacation

Pitch articles for next week

Meet Joy at the coffee shop to work on our novels

Ms. Sophie Brown
Blackbird Farm
7777 Pacific Highway 116
Gravenstein, CA 95472

July 29, 2014

Dear Ms. Sophie Brown,

I understand you have inherited Agnes's chickens.
Please email me to tell me where to send the ones
I was holding for her. You'll want to keep them
separate from the others. Particularly from the ones
Betty has. I'm sure you'll hear from her soon. Best of
luck to you.

Sincerely,
Hortensia James
hjames@APeculiarKindofBird.com

Acknowledgments

From beginning to end, this book was incredibly lucky to have so many people believe in it. Who knew such a little book could hold so much love, support, and thanks?

Thank you (and a never-ending supply of books about chickens) to all the teachers, librarians, and booksellers who found me the books I loved, and who made me realize books are magic. Please keep sharing that magic!

Thank you (and far more books with kids like Sophie) to Chiemi Davis, Malcolm Hightower, Todd Shenk, Kamali'i Yeh Garcia, Nisi Shawl, Cynthia Ward, KT Horning, Diversity in YA, Latin@s in Kid Lit, the Diversity League, and so many others for helping me see things more clearly and think through what to do about it.

Thank you (and all kinds of eggs for the next egg hunt) to my aunts, uncles, cousins, and first cousins, once removed, for teaching me how to tell stories, sharing your stories, listening to my stories, and always laughing in the right places.

Thank you (and vegetables grown by the next three generations) to my grandparents, who always thought anything I did was wonderful and amazing, and always told me so. Every child deserves that feeling.

Thank you (and just a few chickens, won't be any trouble at all) to Jim and Barbara Lakin and Keith, Laura, Henry, and Willa McDaniel for loving stories, too.

Thank you (and a few conversations about something other than books and chickens) to Alene Moroni, Darlene Sluder, and Susan Brown, who believed I could do it (even when I didn't).

Thank you (and something besides Rhode Island Reds) to Hilleary Osheroff, Ben Osheroff, and Carolyn Botts, who had chickens first.

Thank you (and all the chickens I can imagine, and then some) to Terry Jones, Brian Jones, Ross Jones, Betty Jones, and Alicia Mora. I love you guys. I would be someone entirely different without you. Probably much less weird.

Thank you (and a pre-built chicken coop next time) to Eric Lakin for agreeing that, yes, of course we should get chickens of our own, helping me think up chicken superpowers, and coming along on so many adventures.

Thank you (and dozens of eggs with only a little sand) to Vylar Kaftan, Aimee Ogden, Sarah Matanah, Mary Rickert, Christine Puckett, Rick Swann, Sonia Dolores Cook, and Melissa Koosman for feedback along the way, and especially to Jan Waggoner and Barbara Brainin for lending their eyes to other strange notions, too.

Thank you (and your favorite home-cooked migas) to Fernando Clara, Taryn Adam, Alec Adam, Andy Adam, and Kim Baker for helping me get things right.

Thank you (and unusual chickens of your own) to the ladies of EDGE—Emily Kokie, Edith Hope Bishop, Jen Adam, Lish McBride, and Brenna Shanks—for keeping me company along the way. I would never have made it so far without you.

Thank you (and a special glass egg that only you can see inside, and only you know what will hatch out of) to Caroline Stevermer for talking me through it all. I would still be wandering around the middle clucking sadly to myself if not for you.

Thank you (and supernatural Peeps) to SCBWI Western Washington for supporting writers and illustrators, and for introducing me to Mandy.

Thank you (and angry-looking chicks lifting each other with the power of their tiny chick brains) to my agent, Mandy Hubbard, for loving Sophie and her chickens and finding the perfect home for them.

Thank you (clo clo! gackern gackern! coccodè coccodè!) to Taryn Fagerness for loving the chickens and taking them abroad.

Thank you (and a chicken-operated typewriter) to Eric Fitzgerald, Iris Broudy, and Katherine Harrison, whose hard work brought you Sophie's story.

Thank you (and one of Chris's favorite cartoons) to Trish Parcell and Isabel Warren-Lynch, who opened a window into Sophie's world.

Thank you (and her very own copy of *The Hoboken Chicken Emergency*) to Katie Kath. I don't know how you did it, but you drew everyone exactly as they are. Thank you so much for letting us see Sophie and her story as it was meant to be.

Thank you (and unusual chickens even Sophie hasn't seen yet) to my editor, Nancy Siscoe, for understanding exactly who Sophie is and making sure everyone else does, too. I couldn't ask for a better person to save my migas!

And finally, thank you to Marie, Ada, Graybeard, Raven, Ingrid, and Frida for being my muses. May you chase slugs, bulldoze, and dust-bathe forever in Valhalla, Mictlan, or wherever you end up. And may you not develop any unusual superpowers—at least not just yet.

KELLYJONES has worked as a children's librarian and bookseller. She lives near Seattle with her partner and several much-loved chickens, whose imaginary superpowers inspired this, her first novel. You can find her on the Web at curiosityjones.net.

KATIE KATH is a freelance illustrator specializing in books for children. She lives in Georgia, and when she is not working, she is usually baking, singing songs, or planting something. So far, she is chickenless. You can find her at ktkath.com.